THE DANGEROUS DAYS OF
ĐANIEL·X

$1 –

www.**jamespatterson**.co.uk

Also by James Patterson

The Women's Murder Club series

1st to Die
2nd Chance (*with Andrew Gross*)
3rd Degree (*with Andrew Gross*)
4th of July (*with Maxine Paetro*)
The 5th Horseman (*with Maxine Paetro*)
The 6th Target (*with Maxine Paetro*)
7th Heaven (*with Maxine Paetro*)

Maximum Ride series
Maximum Ride: The Angel Experiment
Maximum Ride: School's Out Forever
Maximum Ride: Saving the World and
Other Extreme Sports
The Final Warning

Alex Cross novels
Cat and Mouse
Pop Goes the Weasel
Roses are Red
Violets are Blue
Four Blind Mice
The Big Bad Wolf
London Bridges
Mary, Mary
Cross
Double Cross
Cross Country
(published November 2008)

Detective Michael Bennet series
Step on a Crack (*with Michael Ledwidge*)

Stand-alone thrillers
When the Cradle Blows
Cradle and All
Miracle on 17th Green
(*with Peter de Jonge*)
The Beach House
(*with Peter de Jonge*)
The Jester
(*with Andrew Gross*)
The Lake House
SantaKid
Honeymoon (*with Howard Roughan*)
Lifeguard (*with Andrew Gross*)
Beach Road (*with Peter de Jonge*)
Judge and Jury (*with Andrew Gross*)
The Quickie (*with Michael Ledwidge*)
You've Been Warned
(*with Howard Roughan*)
Sail (published June 2008)

Romance
Suzanne's Diary for Nicholas
Sam's Letter's for Jennifer
Sundays at Tiffany's

Non-fiction
Against All Odds (*with Hal and Cory
Friedman* published September 2008)

THE DANGEROUS DAYS OF
DANIEL·X

James Patterson
and Michael Ledwidge

CORGI BOOKS

THE DANGEROUS DAYS OF DANIEL X
A CORGI BOOK 978 0 552 55848 8

First published in 2008 in Great Britain by Doubleday,
an imprint of Random House Children's Books
A Random House Group Company

Corgi edition published 2009

1 3 5 7 9 10 8 6 4 2

RANDOM HOUSE CHILDREN'S BOOKS
61–63 Uxbridge Road, London W5 5SA

www.kidsatrandomhouse.co.uk
www.rbooks.co.uk

Addresses for companies within
The Random House Group Limited can be found at:
www.randomhouse.co.uk/offices.htm

THE RANDOM HOUSE GROUP Limited Reg. No. 954009

A CIP catalogue record for this book is available from the British Library.

Printed and bound in Australia by Griffin Press

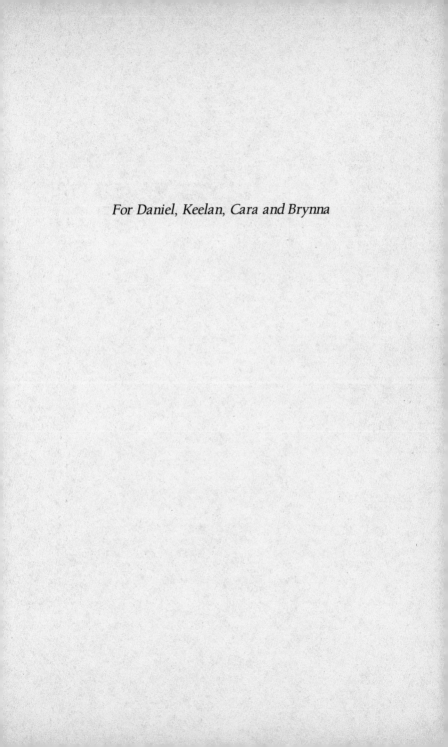

For Daniel, Keelan, Cara and Brynna

THE DANGEROUS DAYS OF
DANIEL·X

True Confessions

IF THIS WERE A MOVIE instead of real life, this would be the part where in a strange, ominous voice I'd say, "Take me to your leader!"

But since *you* are far more important in making a difference in this world than the earth's leaders, and last time I checked on the Internet those leaders seem to have more than enough on their plates, and for the most part I'm not a total dork, I'll just go with a simple "Hi."

My name is Daniel, and this is the first volume of my life story, which, hopefully, will be a very long and distinguished one.

Why should you read it? Very good question.

Maybe because this is your planet, and you have a right to know what's actually happening on it.

And more important, *off* it.

Trust me, there are legions of strange and disturbing creatures out there you probably *don't* want to know about.

Like the fast-breeding creeps with burnt-looking metallic faces and deer horns bristling above hornet noses and stingers, who populate the American Midwest and parts of Europe. Or some very nasty sluglike thingies with jowls like water balloons about to burst all over much of Japan and China, as well as New York City and Vancouver. Plus a host of human-skeletonish freaks with tentacle hair and green multifaceted fly eyes; some white chocolate-colored cretins that look like giant human babies, only with glowing television fuzz for their eyes and mouths; and a praying mantis-looking race with shrunken heads, long red dreadlocks, and a pathetic need to kill, operating in the general area of Texas, Kansas, and Oklahoma.

Maybe I should stop talking, though, before I get too far ahead of myself.

To those of you who feel that you've heard enough, let me say I'm sorry I had to give you a glimpse of what's really out there, and would you please close the cover of this book down tightly on your way out.

Now, the rest of you, I need you to do three important things.

1. Take a deep, deep breath.
2. Disregard everything anyone has ever told you about life on earth.
3. Turn the page.

Prologue

THAT WRETCHED LIST

One

I WISH THAT I didn't sometimes, but I remember everything about that cursed, unspeakably unhappy night
twelve years ago, when I was just three years old and both
my parents were murdered.

I was taking an ordinary can of Play-Doh down from
the playroom shelf when my mom called from the top of
the basement stairs.

"Daniel? Dinner will be ready in five minutes. Time to
start wrapping things up, honey."

Finish? Already? I made a face. *But my latest
masterpiece isn't done yet!*

"Yes, Mom," I called. "One minute. I'm making Play-Doh history down here."

"Of course you are, dear. I would expect nothing less. Love you. Always."

"Love you back, Mom. Always."

In case you've already noticed that I didn't speak like a typical three-year-old, well, you should have seen what I was building.

I stared at the museum-quality replica of the Lighthouse of Alexandria I was trying to finish.

Behind it, all the way to the edge of my worktable, stood matchless reproductions I'd made of the remaining Seven Wonders of the Ancient World:

The Great Pyramid of Giza
The Hanging Gardens of Babylon
The Statue of Zeus at Olympia
The Temple of Artemis at Ephesus
The Mausoleum of Mausolus
The Colossus of Rhodes

I would have liked to do the Cathedral of Notre Dame and the Chrysler Building as well, but I was only allowed one hour of playtime a day.

I squinted suddenly as I spotted what looked like a tiny, flat black seed climbing up the side of my miniature lighthouse, and really moving too.

Whoa there, little guy! Where do you think you're motoring to?

It was an Arthropoda Arachnida Acari Metastigmata, I thought, recalling the phylum, class, order, and suborder of the tiny creature at a glance. A tick. A young male dog tick, to be exact.

"Hey, little fella," I whispered to the tick. "You on a sightseeing tour?"

Two things happened next, almost simultaneously. Two very odd and unforgettable things.

There was a strange shimmering at the back of my bright, turquoise-blue eyes.

And the tick slowly rose onto its hind legs and said, "Hey, Daniel, my brother, you do real nice work. *Cool lighthouse!*"

Two

I LAUGHED HYSTERICALLY as the lickety-split-quick tick crawled higher and higher on the lighthouse. Well, technically I was the one making it crawl, and tell jokes.

With my mind!

Yes, you heard that correctly. I was causing the tick to do tricks and also talk. It's a talent I have. Long story. *Good* story, but not for right now. Something earth-shattering was about to happen at our house.

Anyway, I had the little fellow give a wave before it flipped forward and did a one-clawed handstand on the top of the lighthouse.

And at that exact, unforgettable instant, I suddenly flew back off the bench as a wall-shaking explosion detonated in the room above my head.

Something enormous had just crashed into the kitchen! *Was it a freight train? A plane?*

A sick feeling ripped through my stomach. *Where was my mom?*

"The List!" I now heard a deep, strangled voice roar from the kitchen above. "You think you can hide it from *me!* I know you have The List. *And I want it! NOW!*"

I climbed to my feet, my mouth open, my eyes wide and locked onto the ceiling.

"Don't hurt us! Please!" my mother sobbed. "Who are you? What list?"

"Wait, wait. Hold on," I heard my father say. "Lower the gun, my friend. I'll get The List for you. I have it nearby."

"The List is *here?*" The deep voice loomed once again. "Right here? In this pathetic little hovel in Kansas, of all places?"

"Yes. Now if you'll just lower the—"

I fell to the floor again as a string of deafening explosions drowned out my father's voice. *Shooting,* I thought, my eyes clenched shut, my hands flying to my ears. *An Opus 24/24,* I realized with the same instantaneous knowledge that I'd had about the

Arthropoda Arachnida Acari Metastigmata, the dog tick.

Then I heard my father call out, "We love you, Daniel. *Always*."

The clanging echo of the shots hung in the silence after the Opus finally stopped.

"Stay right there. Don't get up, either of you. *As if you could*," the stranger said with a nasty laugh. "I'll go find The List myself."

Mom? I thought, tears flooding down my cheeks. *Dad?*

Then another terrible thought entered my mind, and it was bright and urgent as a neon sign.

"The aliens are here," I whispered, and reached up and clicked off the basement light. I prepared to be eaten, or maybe worse.

Three

I WAS TREMBLING and pressing my small, vulnerable body up against an old water heater, petrified about what might have just happened to my mom and dad, when a beam of violet-tinged light shone down the stairs into the basement.

And then I saw it—a six-and-a-half-foot-tall praying mantis. At least it had taken that terrible form tonight.

From behind the water heater, I stared in horror at the creature's long, grossly bulging, plum-colored body, its small, almost shrunken head, its large, liquid-black eyes. What a foul beast! It had long, stringy red dreadlocks hanging down between its antennae, and a dull black metal assault rifle cradled in its sharply jointed arms.

"I know you're down here, boy," the xxl-sized insect said with a slow, horrifying roll of its stalklike neck. "I am called The Prayer, and there is very little that The Prayer does not know. If you come to me now, I may go easy on you. *May*. But I do hereby promise, cross my heart and hope to live forever, if you continue to make me play this silly game of hide-and-seek, you are going to learn the meaning of the word *punishment*."

This abomination, this beast that dared call itself The Prayer, proceeded to tear the basement apart, obviously looking for The List. Powered by its massive legs it suddenly leaped upstairs and trashed the rest of the house —screeching, *"LIST! LIST! LIST! LIST!"*

Then it was back in my playspace, looking for me, no doubt angrier and hungrier than ever.

The Prayer smiled eerily then, flashing jagged yellow, broken-bottle-shard teeth. It covered fifteen feet of room with a single hop.

"Game over, you pathetic little pukemeister. Maybe *you* know where The List is. *Do you? DO YOU?*"

That's when I realized that behind the thick wall of fear, my mind was actually trying to save me.

Of course, I thought. I had a plan, a shred of hope that could salvage my life.

The Prayer swung its evil-looking head around the side of the water heater.

And found *absolutely nothing!*

Four
———

THE REPUGNANT FREAK GASPED with surprise and outrage. "*What?*" it screeched at the top of its voice range. "Not possible! I smelled you there a second ago!"

Well, technically I was still right there. I looked cross-eyed at my new beaklike hypostome as I scurried away on my eight new clawed legs. The answer to my immediate problem had been straightforward: *all I needed to do was make myself less conspicuous to the murderous beast.*

Do you follow what had just happened? The full significance of it? It's important.

You see, my abilities didn't stop at being able to make ticks talk and do tricks.

Now I *was* the tick. I had transformed myself.

Towering above me like a skyscraper, The Prayer opened its razor-sharp jaws and there was a bubbling-wet, sickening sound. Then a jet of jellylike blue flame shot from his mouth. The basement walls, carpet, and ceiling caught fire in the blink of my eyes.

"Take that, you little nothing! I flame-broil my meat. Like Burger King! And Beelzebub!"

Still in tiny tick form, I raced away from the smoke and scorching heat until I was crushed against the basement's concrete foundation wall, which now seemed as big as a cliff to me.

I reached up tentatively with one of my claws. Some good news at last. My claw stuck to the concrete like superglue.

Next I was scampering up the wall behind The Prayer's head. Then I jumped and landed smack-dab in the center of the alien's greasy, dreadlocked hair.

I locked my hypostome down tight like a seat belt on a strand of his hair just as the homicidal Prayer jumped effortlessly to the top of the burning basement stairs again.

There I got a horrific, never-to-be-forgotten look at my mom and dad lying facedown on the kitchen floor. I knew they were dead and there was nothing I could do for them. I *knew* it in my heart and soul. I just couldn't believe it yet, couldn't accept it.

Then The Prayer smashed through the kitchen window and burst into the night.

"FAILURE! FAILURE! FAILURE!" it bellowed. *"I hate failure! WHERE IS THE LIST?"*

Something struck my head then, the end of a tree branch maybe, and I found myself flying through the cold air. The breath was knocked out of me, and I landed hard on the packed dirt floor of the woods behind our farmhouse.

I was a three-year-old boy again. *Transformed.* No longer a tick. I stood and turned back, and stared in disbelief and terror that could find no voice at that awful moment.

Already our house was a blazing shell of its former self. My mom and dad were dead and being incinerated inside. There was the sound of glass shattering as the upstairs window to my bedroom blew out with the heat.

Then, for a long time, there was the roar of the flames, and my soft, little-boy cries as I stood alone in the world for the first time, orphaned and homeless.

I recalled a song my mom used to sing to me: *Star light, star bright. First star I see tonight.* She and my dad loved the skies and the stars.

And I remember thinking, very clearly, as if I had suddenly grown up on that horrifying, unforgettable night: *I know where The List is—my father has taken me to see it many times. Maybe for just this reason.*

And I know what it is: The List of Alien Outlaws on Terra Firma.

And I know who I am: Daniel, son of Graff, son of Terfdron—the Alien Hunter.

No last name, just Daniel X.

I have to tell you one more thing about that night. I must get it out.

Even though I was only three years old, I am ashamed that I didn't fight The Prayer to the death.

DANIEL X, ALIEN HUNTER

Chapter 1

TWELVE YEARS HAVE PASSED. I'm fifteen now. All grown up, sort of.

When I tell you that I've seen it all and done it all, I'm not lying or boasting—though sometimes I wish I were, and that I lived a normal life in some place like Peoria, Illinois, or Red Bank, New Jersey.

Since the death of my mom and dad, and in my years as an Alien Hunter—up to and including the present moment of extraordinary jeopardy—I've been kidnapped by faceless metallic humanoids. *Twice.*

I've been chased and caught by a shape shifting protoplasm in London who wanted to make me into a jelly sandwich, without the bread.

I have done hand-to-antennae combat with an entire civilization of insects in Mexico City, Cuernavaca, and Acapulco.

I've had my face run over again and again—for days—by self-replicating machines that were about to take over Detroit. *And wait—it gets worse.*

A billion or so "little wailing mouths" connected by an electrical network to a single mind—I don't know how else to describe them—ate and digested me in Hamburg, Germany.

I will *not* tell you how I got out of that one.

But this particular creature, *currently right in my face,* was really, really testing my limits, and my patience.

Chapter 2

ITS NAME WAS ORKNG JLLFGNA and it was Number 19 on The List of Alien Outlaws. I had caught up with it in Portland, Oregon, after a month-long search through Canada and the Pacific Northwest, with a near-miss capture attempt in Seattle.

More to the point, it was at the moment blocking my escape out of a disgusting sewage pipe underneath the fair city of Portland, somewhere, I believe, between the Rose Garden Arena and PGE Park.

Orkng was actually living in the sewer, and on this particular night, at around two o'clock, I had come on an extermination mission. I despised this kidnapper of the elderly and their pets (dog liver is a delicacy on its hideous home planet). I can best describe this alien freak as part man, part jellyfish, part chain saw.

"You're very impressive and scary, Orkng—may I call you Orkng?" I asked.

"Is that your *last wish?*" The creature growled and then spun its immense buzz saw toward my eyes.

"Oh, I hope not. Say, I've read you have Level 4 strength. True or false?"

Orkng took out a quarter and bent it in half—*with its eyelid!*

"And you're a shape-shifter too?" I pretended to marvel, or grovel, I guess you could call it.

Rather than a simple yes or no, Orkng changed itself into a kind of squid with a human face featuring a mouth with hundreds of teeth.

The entire changing process took about five seconds.

Interesting, I thought. *Could be something to work with here.*

"That's it? That's all you can do?" I asked the squid thing. "I came down into this sewer for that?"

"That's nothing, you little chump." Orkng snickered, frowned, and burped up something resembling a dozen oysters sans the half shells.

Once again, it began to change—only this time, I

leaped right inside the confluence of shifting molecules and atoms and photons. How brave, or dumb, was that?

How creative?

Then I used my Level 3 strength for all it was worth. I punched and I kicked gaping holes into the still-unformulated creature. I fought as if my life depended on it—which it obviously did. Then I began shredding the murderous monster into tiny pieces with my hands.

It was terrible and gruesome and took hours to accomplish, and I hated every second of it, every shred.

But when the deed was done, I was able to cross Number 19 off my List, and I was one step closer to Number 1—The Prayer, who had killed my mom and dad.

All in a night's work in the sewers of Portland.

Chapter 3

THE SUN WAS JUST COMING UP—well, the grayish-white smudge that passes for a sun in forever-overcast Portland—as I lumbered through my rental apartment's front door and plopped down on the couch.

I crossed my muddy boots on the coffee table and yawned as I opened the morning's *Oregonian*.

As exhausted as my body was, my mind was still wired about the night before. I jumped up and went to my computer. I pulled up The List of Alien Outlaws and checked to see who was naughty and had been recently exterminated. *Yessiree, Number 19 was no longer on the boards!*

This was, in fact, the same List that The Prayer had been trying to find that fateful day twelve years ago. When I was thirteen, I finally revisited the burnt-down farmhouse where my poor parents had been incinerated. After several days of searching, I found The List—buried under mud and rocks in the rather picturesque brook that ran behind the house.

The List was on a computer—the one now before me, which is thin as a notepad and probably five hundred years in advance of anything currently offered by Apple or ibm. When I first opened it, I discovered that it contained the names, full description, and approximate whereabouts of the known outlaw aliens currently roaming the earth. And trust me on this: *they are out there, watching and studying us.*

There was also a disturbing message for me from my mom and dad. If I was reading it, the note said, I was to replace them. I was to be the Alien Hunter. I would have to learn how mostly by myself.

As I was pondering this troubling episode from my past, the front doorbell rang.

Not good. I wasn't expecting anyone—*I'm never expecting anyone.* I don't really like visitors, which is ironic, since I'm lonely most of the time and I adore people, actually.

Oh, no! I thought, realizing who it was. And when I say

I knew who it was, I'm not saying I had a really good hunch. I *knew* it as fact.

We'll get into that in greater detail after I get rid of my visitors.

The police.

Chapter 4

PARANOIA ALERT! I told myself.

Standing on my doorstep were two hulking, none-too-happy-looking Portland pd uniforms. Their radios were squawking loudly beside their holstered 9 millimeter handguns.

"Hey, champ," the older-looking of the two said. "Parents home?" Interesting question. And a real conversation stopper given my history.

"Uh," I said. "Yeah. I mean, of course . . . but they're . . . pretty busy right now. Maybe I could help you? Or you could come back later?"

"Later?" he said. "That's not exactly going to work with our busy schedule. See, we're from the Runaway Juvenile Unit. One of your neighbors called us. Said she sees you coming in and out at all times of the day and night, and no sign of your parents anywhere. So if they're too *busy* to come out and talk to the police, you can come with us. We'll straighten this out at the precinct house. That be okay? You following me so far?"

I'd dealt with the runaway units of several police departments in my travels over the previous couple of years. They were usually pretty cool people who were, for the most part, trying to help troubled kids. For the most part, *but not right now.*

I guess I could have told these two the truth. That I wasn't a runaway but an Alien Hunter in town to take care of an important extermination. But I don't know. They didn't look ready to hear about the timely end of Orkng Jllfgna down in Portland's sewers.

"Okay, kid. Time's up now. Let's get moving," the older guy said. "Charade's over."

Charade, I thought, nodding. *What a good idea.*

Chapter 5

NOW PAY ATTENTION, because this is important, and also way out of the ordinary. I suspect you've never seen, or heard about, or read anything like this before.

The older patrolman was fingering the cuffs hanging off his Sam Browne belt when a loud clatter of pots and pans came from the kitchen.

The game was on! Here goes . . .

"Daniel, who's there?" a woman's voice called. "I'll be out in a minute, after I flip these pancakes. Daniel? I'm talking to you!"

The look of surprise on the cops' faces was priceless,

actually, almost worth the stress of the moment.

"Want to join us for a late breakfast, gentlemen? *Pancakes?*" I said, with a "you know how moms are" look.

A door opened down the hall and a groggy-looking man in his forties stepped out wearing a ratty bathrobe, baggy pajama bottoms, flip-flops, and a Portland Trail Blazers T-shirt.

"Hey, what's all the noise about?" he said. "Hey, guys, what's up? Awful early for visitors."

"Officer Wirtschafter, Portland pd," the older cop said.

"Hey, Dad," I said. "Sorry to wake you. The police think—*I'm a runaway?*"

"A runaway?" My dad yawned and grabbed the edge of the door. "Well, I guess not. I'm Daniel's dad. Harold Hopper."

"Okay, Mr. Hopper, but I'm afraid there's another problem," Officer Wirtschafter said sourly. "Portland has a truancy reduction ordinance. All kids between seven and eighteen are required to attend school. It's nine-thirty now. Your son obviously isn't in school."

"Maybe he has the German measles," my dad said. "What kind of school does he have to attend?"

The cops exchanged a "we got a live one" look. Actually, quite the opposite was true.

"That would be, uh, high school," the older gentleman answered.

"High school, sure. Well, that would be a real waste of time," my dad said and began to laugh. I laughed along with him as he put his arm around my shoulder.

My mom came in then, wiping her hands on her apron. My mom is blond and tall and, if I do say so myself, quite the looker. In a very dignified, mom sort of way.

"Oh, I'm so sorry, officers. My husband is a jokester sometimes. And slow to get to the point. Daniel doesn't need to go to school anymore."

Chapter 6

"MA'AM, EVERYBODY NEEDS to go to school," the cop said.

My mom continued. "Daniel went to high school—when he was ten. He has an IQ, oh, somewhere in the 190s. He graduated from MIT last year. Our Danny has a degree in molecular engineering. We're very proud of him."

"Is that so?" the cop said, dubious. "In that case, if you would just go and get his diploma. College *or* high school would be fine."

"No problem," my dad said, crossing his arms as he

stood in front of me. "Right after we see yours. That sound fair to you?"

"You're a funny guy," the cop said. "You should be on Comedy Central. But I'm not joking about the diploma."

"You'll see his diploma when we see a warrant," my dad said with a winky smile. "Now you and Silent Bob there can leave. Wouldn't want you to catch the measles."

"It'll actually be fun hauling you, your wife, and your 'genius' son in when we come back with that warrant," the cop snarled.

He and his partner turned around and left in a huffy hurry.

"I don't think he was kidding," my dad said to me as we stood in the doorway and watched the Portland pd car squeal away from our building.

"I know, Dad. I'll be out of here before they get to the end of our street. I'm going after Number 6 next. Ergent Seth."

My mom winced. "Oh Daniel, are you sure about that? Number 6 might be way too much, way too soon."

I stared at her sadly. She looked real pretty in her apron. There was even a dab of pancake batter on her cheek. "Trust me, I've studied The List carefully, Mom. He's the next one. Ergent Seth has to go. Now. He's on a terrible rampage in California."

Then I closed my eyes. I took a breath and let it out

slowly, and when I opened my eyes again, my mom and dad were gone.

They were gone because I was the one who created them in the first place. I fashioned them into existence out of my memory—just to run interference with the cops. Like I said, a charade. And a pretty good one too.

Now you know a little more about me.

Freaky, huh?

You have no idea.

Chapter 7

HERE'S THE THING that I have to share with you.

I have these powers, and I don't know exactly how I got them. I can create things, for example. Like my parents. Of course, technically they're not my parents. My real parents are dead. My imagined parents are probably just mental projections that I make real.

And when I say *real*, I mean it. When I manifest my mom and dad, they're as real as you or me. Right down to their dna.

How do I do it? Good question.

I don't know the specifics, but what I do know is that

at its most microscopic, most subatomic level, everything in the universe—matter, people, the air, all the elements, and even energy—is made up of the same basic materials. *And I was born with a strange ability to rearrange the material at will.*

I know what you might be thinking. I can just snap my fingers and what I want is there, but it's not really like that. Not at all.

There's only so much I can create, for a limited period. I have to be really calm, and concentrate like you wouldn't believe. If I'm tired or cranky, forget it—it won't work. Plus there seems to be a mass limit. Or sometimes I seem to run up against a mental block of some kind. One time I tried to create a really cool, flaming red Ferrari, but nothing happened.

Some things are easy to create. My mom and dad, for one. I do them a lot. When I'm afraid or lonely. They're like a recipe you've done over and over again until you can do it in your sleep.

I'm pretty fast too. I'm talking about movement now. One time a New Jersey state trooper tried to arrest me for hitchhiking, and as he started to close the cuff on my wrist, I reached out, grabbed his hand, and pulled it forward so fast he actually cuffed himself.

Oh, and I've caught birds. Not slowpokes like chickens

either. I plucked a passing sparrow out of the air—gently—just to see if I could. I could.

I'm strong, especially for someone who's five ten, 140 pounds. Not strong enough to lift a car, but I could probably flip one in a pinch. I can influence people. Sort of an instant hypnosis type of thing. And I can sometimes tell what's going to happen before it happens. Like knowing that there were cops at the door.

But this is the most important part. Life-and-death stuff. Don't let anybody tell you any different: there *are* aliens on this planet. They've been here millions, maybe hundreds of millions of years. They were on the earth before man, even. And most of these creepy-crawlers are seriously homicidal lunatics.

Number 19 was a horror show and a half—but Number 6, my next target, was actually plotting to change everything about life on Earth. And I don't mean he was going to bring in universal health care and solve global warming. I'm not talking homicidal, I'm talking *genocidal*. Number 6 wanted to take over Earth and destroy every life-form, then recolonize with freaks from his own planet. That's why I had to go after Number 6 now, before he got on a roll . . .

One more thing I need to cover. There might be some good aliens here. I've never met one, but hey, never say never, right? The one thing I know to be true, there are definitely bad ones. I don't think I can stress that part enough.

But wait a second.

This is going to blow your mind. It did mine.

Actually, I have met a good alien.

In the mirror. In every mirror I look at.

I'm pretty sure I'm an alien too.

Chapter 8

I LEFT PORTLAND, heading south on a Greyhound bus. Truthfully, I prefer the train, but train company clerks usually ask questions if you look like you're a minor, which I do, which I *am*.

I tend to try to stay as paranoid as I can, and that's because I'm always being followed. I don't like the idea of my name, or even an alias, floating around in somebody's database. In fact, *right now* I'm afraid I'm being followed. But I try not to think about it too much. Too depressing and disturbing.

On the positive side, the bus was only half full—

believe me, few things in life are worse than a lengthy ride on a crowded bus, except maybe confronting an alien with an appetite—but even so, I only took the Greyhound as far south as Grants Pass, a town thirty miles north of the California border.

I could have gone all the way to la, my next destination—Number 6's home base—but fourteen hours riding the dog is my personal limit.

I laid out my Rand McNally in the back of a McDonald's across from the bus station. I wanted to see if there was a way to Southern California besides Interstate 5 so that I could be a little more off the beaten path. Right away I spotted another, skinnier road, 199, heading for the California coast. The fact that I'd never seen the Pacific before settled it for me.

Oregon's rain seemed to instantly turn to Northern California fog as I put the McDonald's behind me and stuck out my thumb.

I don't recommend hitching, by the way. *Do not*. There are some pretty sick wack-a-doos out there. If I hadn't had the means to protect myself and the urgent need to cover my tracks, I would have stayed on the bus.

But you come across some good people on the road too. I actually caught my first lift from a couple of them, two nuns heading for a retreat house in Kerby. They were wearing habits, and I thought they would give me a sermon or something, but all we did was talk about the Mariners baseball team and its slim-to-none chances of making the al wild card. Even better, they didn't ask me where I was going, so I didn't have to lie to them.

"God bless you," they said, as they let me off. How nice was that? Maybe they had a sixth sense that I was about to need some extra blessings.

Chapter 9

IT WAS GETTING DARK an hour later when I came across a card-carrying, charter member of the wack-a-doo species. To put it mildly.

I didn't mind so much that the pickup truck I stuck out my thumb at didn't stop. It was the can of Busch beer that sailed out of his passenger window that I found quite unnecessary. It probably would have shattered the bone structure of my face if I didn't have pretty good reflexes. I ducked at the last second and watched as the full can exploded with a foamy hiss against the trunk of a pine tree.

I decided I needed to teach that idiot truck driver a lesson about highway safety and etiquette.

I stared at the can and *willed* the spilled beer back into it. Then I sealed the crack and pop-top, and holding it in my hand like a runner's baton, I started after the truck.

It took me a full ten seconds to catch up. I could have done it in less, but Busch boy was doing a hundred or so, and the roads were windy that day.

I gave the surprised driver a big wink as I drew alongside his pickup's open window. "What the . . . how the?" he yelled over the howl of the wind.

"Hey, I think you dropped something," I said, and I tossed the beer can into his lap. "Don't drink and drive, you useless dink."

I was acting pretty smug—until I realized that my ability to sense danger was not nearly as advanced as my super speed and strength.

Because suddenly it wasn't a beer-guzzling fool who was driving the truck—it was a plug-ugly alien with a series of wide eyes that went all the way around his head, at least a couple of noses, and dueling mouths equipped with nothing but sharp fangs, dozens of them.

Chapter 10

"SO *WHO'S* CHASING *WHOM?*" he asked with one of the mouths. "And which of my mouths gets to take a huge bite out of you first?" he asked with the other.

Speed is the key, I thought—and still keeping up with the truck, I stuck finger after finger into at least a dozen of the creep's eyes. Then I held on to both of his ears and yelled, "Who sent you after me? I want to know right now!"

The cretin actually started laughing. "You're getting *ahead* of yourself, punk," he said with one mouth. "I'm not *after* you, I'm still to come," he said with the other.

"Say again," I told him.

"Number 6 sent me, and you better go back the way you came. You better run the other way! You get it? You turn around, you boogie, or you die a horrible death in the near future."

Then the voice changed before I knew what was happening. "Ow, ow, ow, ow, ow! Please let me go," he wailed. "Please, *please,* I've learned my lesson!"

And I knew why—because suddenly he was the truck driver again, and I was practically tearing the poor knucklehead's ears off.

"Drive safe," I said, and let him go.

So—Number 6 somehow knew I was coming. What other powers did Ergent Seth have that were as impressive as my own?

Chapter 11

BY TEN O'CLOCK, completely wiped and with still no sign of civilization, I decided to call it a night.

I stepped off the road into the dark woods, kicking myself for staying up late to watch *The Blair Witch Project* a couple nights before. I found a level clearing about thirty yards in that was as good a spot to camp as any.

I opened my minitent and made a little fire. Then I sat beneath the northern stars, propped against a fir tree, cold hot dog in one hand, warm Gatorade in the other. Ahhh, the great outdoors. Could it get much better?

I hoped so, because it was pretty lonely, actually. And

scary, considering that I'm often hunted by aliens.

That's when I heard a bunch of footsteps just outside the firelight. *Uh-oh.*

"Quit tripping me, doofus." I heard a girl's voice.

"That's not me. It's Willy," said a boy. "You know what a klutz he is."

"No, it's not. It's Dana," said another boy. "I'm not a klutz."

"You are *such* a klutz."

"Hello? Does anyone notice that it's like pitch-black?" said yet another girl's voice.

"No, Emma, we didn't notice that."

"Hey, guys," I finally called out to the intruders. "What took you so long?"

My best friends—in the whole universe—had just arrived.

Let the party begin.

Chapter 12

MY BUDDIES WILLY, Joe-Joe, Emma, and Dana had come to keep me company. Just like I do with my parents, I create them. And if you think about it, *creating* is the best superpower of them all. It's a whole lot better than being part *spider*.

"Survival training. I love it," Willy said, punching fists with me. "The great outdoors! The Pacific Northwest! Wow! You know how to travel, Daniel."

Stocky and headstrong, with shoulder-length black hair, Willy is around my age—fifteen or so. He's always ready, willing, and able to try anything, and mix it up with any *thing*. If anyone enjoys chasing down aliens as much as I do, it's Willy. The guy is fearless, loyal to a fault, and all heart.

"Chex Mix! Righteous!" Joe said, plopping down and snatching the bag out of my hand. Joe-Joe, on the other hand, is more like *all stomach*. Which is crazy, because he's super skinny. He's also messy, an athlete at nothing but competitive eating, and the most sarcastic, funniest motormouth I know.

"Oh, wow!" Emma said, twirling around. "Spruce, cedars, Douglas firs, cypresses. Amazing! I love it here. Great spot, Daniel."

Emma's a year younger than Willy, and she's his sister. She's also our little group's Earth Mother. Compassionate to a fault, Emma loves two things: the planet Earth and all of its animals, even the insects.

"Hey, *you*," Dana said smiling at me with a jaunty shake of her head. "Decided to take us camping, huh? Interesting. I mean, heat and indoor plumbing, how overrated are they?"

I smiled back, my mouth suddenly dry.

What can I say about Dana? She's tall, with pin-straight blond hair that flows like a waterfall of flame down her back. She's probably the most beautiful girl I've ever seen—just my opinion, of course—but the neat part is that hands down, Dana's the most genuine person I've met. No ego, no big head, no agenda.

I have a crush on Dana so bad that it makes me physically shake sometimes. It's embarrassing! Like when I look into her eyes, which are in the blue family, somewhere between chambray and shaved ice.

I stared at her in the firelight across from me and felt my wet, cold carcass instantly warm up.

"Way to go, Daniel!" Joe said, his cheeks bloated with Chex Mix, wincing as he sat on a hard root. "Sweet spot you picked here, buddy. I mean, I love the cold by itself, but *wet,* too? And lousy grub."

"Joe's actually right for once," Willy said, whittling a stick into an arrow with my pocketknife. "This place is a dump."

"A dump?" Emma said, outraged. "The Pacific Northwest is like one of the biologically richest areas in North America. Maybe in all the temperate areas of the world. Besides all of the coniferous growth, it's home to the mourning dove and the western fence lizard."

"Hey, you're right, Emma. This eco-biosystem thingy is really starting to grow on me," Joe said. "In fact . . ."

Joe got down on one knee in front of the Douglas fir beside him and mimicked opening a jewelry box. "Will you marry me?" he said to the tree. "Seriously. I love you, tree."

"Enough, clown boy," Dana said to Joe. "I call Trivial Pursuit."

Chapter 13

WHAT CAN I SAY? We like to play board games. All right, so we're a little nerdy. And since this whole scene was my creation, we could bend the rules any way we wanted.

"First question, Dana," Emma said, drawing a card. "Category is entertainment. Who played the role of George Bailey in Frank Capra's Christmas classic, *It's a Wonderful Life*? I know you know it, girl."

Joe finished my Gatorade and gave a deafening burp. "Samuel L. Jackson," he said. "No, wait. It was Mini-Me."

"Jimmy Stewart," Dana said.

"You go, girl," said Emma. "Next question—Joe. Category is theoretical physics. In quantum electrodynamics, what is the full scattering amplitude the sum of?"

"Theoretical physics!" Joe said, outraged. "E equals MC squared. How should I know? Let me see that card!"

"Incorrect," Emma said. "Daniel, your turn. Science and nature. What does *elephant* mean in Latin?"

"An *elephant* question!" Joe said, rolling his eyes. "I get the thermo whatzit and Daniel, *the elephant nerd,* gets an elephant question? Besides, he knows Latin."

"And about a hundred other languages," said Dana.

"Huge arch," I said, ignoring them. "*Ele* means arch and *phant* means huge."

After we played Trivial Pursuit for about an hour more, I finally said, "You know what, guys? I think I'm gonna hit the sack. I've had a long, hard one today."

"Where we headed this time?" Will said.

"LA," I said. "On the trail of Number 6. He's nasty, and I think he's getting ready to make a big strike at Terra Firma. He already sent a henchman to warn me off."

"la, cool!" Joe said. "Number 6, cooler. The scarier the better. The few, the proud, *us.*"

"You got my back tonight?" I said to Willy as I stood up and stretched my arms toward the moon.

"Anything gets close to this campfire that Joe can't

eat," Willy said, punching my leg as I stepped past him, "you're going to be the first to know."

Dana poked her head down close as I slid into my sleeping bag. She looked incredible in the pitch-black— but in the firelight, *wow!*

"Hey, you," I said.

"Just wanted to say good night," she whispered, leaning in. "You handsome devil, you. You are gorgeous, you know? Good night, Dannyboy." The last thing I felt was the sweet brush of her lips on my cheek.

And then I was dreaming.

Chapter 14

WELCOME TO MY NIGHTMARES!

I have these incredible, vivid dreams that are like high-definition virtual reality. The one I had that night was a recurring one where I was a warrior in a world like Middle Earth in *The Lord of the Rings*, or maybe *300*. I was on a battlefield, holding a shining sword, surrounded by a Yankee Stadium-sized crowd of seething, hopelessly evil creatures. They were heavily armed, and every one of them was there to fight me. They all wanted their piece, but especially the real treasure—my brain.

I turned to try to run but then saw that Willy, Joe,

Emma, and Dana were at my side. "We've got your back—well, kinda!" Willy yelled.

And then, as always, I saw The Prayer coming at me.

And, as always, Number 1 killed me! Set me on fire, cooked me to medium rare, and then ate me.

I really, really, really hope I haven't just given away the ending of this story.

Chapter 15

A DAY LATER I arrived in LA, hot on the trail of Number 6—or maybe he was hot on my trail, hard to tell. As I said earlier, his name was Ergent Seth, and according to The List, he lived somewhere called Malibu. The depraved entity was believed to be in the film industry, which made sense if you think about some of the movies they make these days.

I created my mom and dad again, and this time included my sister Pork Chop (Brenda), to help me rent a house in Glendale, which is a suburb of LA.

The nicest thing about the rent-a-house was its

gleaming gourmet kitchen. After a long-overdue shower and a quick stop at the supermarket, I spent the next two hours cracking eggs, chopping onions, grinding meat, selecting herbs and spices.

Cooking is a hobby and a passion of mine. It calms me, helps me unwind, and, hey, I'm fifteen. I eat like a truck driver.

I kept my parents and even Pork Chop around for dinner and some nice chitchat. I decided it was Italian night, spaghetti, sausage, and meatballs to be precise, but done the real way. I like to go the whole nine. Top-quality, freshly ground beef, veal, pork, and pancetta, a type of Italian bacon. Roma tomatoes and extra virgin olive oil for the sauce. Fresh pasta. Fresh basil and oregano and Romano and mozzarella cheeses to top it all off.

I'd learned the wonders of authentic Italian on a trip to Sicily six months earlier. I wasn't there on a vacation, unfortunately, but to take out Number 24, a homicidal, gun-running alien known as Bang, Bang, Doom, who lived in a heavily guarded villa outside Palermo. Beautiful digs, great views.

After dinner, I was thinking about making a fire. Then I was going to catch up on reading this novel I'd picked up in Portland, *Water for Elephants*. A honey of a story!

From the looks of ecstasy on my family's faces around the granite kitchen island, I knew I'd nailed the meal.

Even Pork Chop shut her motormouth for a few seconds and shoveled in dinner.

"Thanks for helping me out, guys," I said, lowering my fork and raising my Pellegrino in a toast. "Here's to the best family in the world."

Even though you're not real.

Chapter 16

AFTER DESSERT my mom hung back in the kitchen as my dad and sister went to see what was on tv. Pork Chop stopped the remote on an old *Simpsons* rerun, her favorite show.

"I saw The List of Alien Outlaws," my mom said, sliding me her half-eaten slice of cake. "You're going after Ergent Seth for sure? Number 6. Is that true, Daniel?"

I couldn't help but detect the concern in her voice, and in her eyes as well. Kind of sweet, but hey, I'm not three years old anymore. And I'm battle tested.

"That's right," I said, trying to act nonchalant. "It's no biggie."

"You are aware that this is the first time you've gone after a monster in the top ten."

"I hadn't thought of it in exactly that way," I said. "You're suggesting that things are going to get more dangerous for me?"

"That's putting it very mildly," she said. "You make the slightest mistake, the tiniest misstep, Number 6 isn't going to give you a chance to make a second one. Look what happened to your father and me. You could *die* this time. Do you understand what that means?"

I nodded slowly, remembering the worst night of my life, when I was three. The screams of my mom and dad, the gunfire blasting through our house. The fear as I crouched, cornered in the darkness as The Prayer came down the stairs.

"Thanks for the wake-up call, Mom. I'll be careful. And clever and resourceful, and devious if that's what it takes. Number 6 is up to something . . . *world shaking*. I have to do this."

Then my mother did something that I think moms must have been invented for. She hugged me hard and kissed me on the forehead. She knew exactly what I needed somehow. Then she pinched my cheek, which she always does. I've never understood it, but I let her get away with it every time.

Chapter 17

"OKAY, GUYS," I said with a yawn. "Thanks for all your help. And counsel. I've got a big day ahead. Murderous aliens to catch, you know."

"Daniel," said my father. "You're not ready for Number 6. *I* wouldn't have been ready for Number 6. Even your mother and I working together would be no match for this fiend."

"Wait a second. No way!" Pork Chop said as my mom put her arm around her shoulder. "We can't leave now! There's still five minutes of my show left. I've never even seen this episode before.

I want to see what happens to Sideshow Bob. *Mom!*"

But then they were gone, and I clicked off the tv set.

I stood for a moment, taking in all the peace and quiet. And loneliness, I thought, looking at the empty plates on the counter.

And fear.

And paranoia.

After I finished cleaning up, I decided to crash right there on the couch.

I closed my eyes—and almost instantly I saw The Prayer. "Ergent Seth will destroy you," he said. "Go back to Portland. Join the circus. Get a girlfriend if you can. Get an identity, Daniel X. Have a life. For a little while. Until I come for you."

Great. Now my biggest enemies were parenting me. Guess that's what can happen when you're all alone in the world.

Chapter 18

I DIDN'T SLEEP very well that night, barely an hour. No big surprise there, I guess. Who needs sleep anyway?

It was a quarter to eight the next morning when I reached Glendale High School. I wanted to try to blend into the community, and especially avoid a truant squad run-in like the one in Portland. So I decided I'd better at least sign up for school.

Plus, I'm sure I didn't want to admit it then, but maybe The Prayer's words in my dream were starting to get to me. *Until I come for you.*

I stopped by the front steps, taking in the swirl of

relatively carefree students unloading from the buses and minivans. I was a little skittish, but also excited at the thought of hanging out with people my own age.

I hadn't been to high school in, well, *ever,* actually.

"Hi, I'm Daniel Hopper," I said to the secretary behind the counter in the main office. "My mom said she faxed over my paperwork. Is it okay?"

The middle-aged woman checked a clipboard on the desk behind her.

"Oh, yes. Here you are, Daniel. Did you bring documentation from your last?"

Not likely. "Right here," I said, handing over a forged birth certificate and Social Security card. The previous school records I'd invented were from a fictitious private school in Haneyville, Kentucky.

"Welcome to Glendale High, Daniel," she said, pointing at a door beside her. "Go inside and see Vice Principal Marshman. He'll help you schedule your classes."

Chapter 19

I THANKED THE SECRETARY and opened the vice principal's door in a cautious, respectful way. Mr. Marshman was a wide, flabby, middle-aged fellow, and the school's head football coach, I gathered from the framed articles covering the wall behind his wrecking ball of a head. He was on the phone when I entered. "I know you booked the bus for the debating team, Leopoldo. But how many times are my guys going to get the chance to go to UCLA and watch the Bruins practice? I gotta go. End of debate. You lose."

"Hi, I'm—" I started as he hung up the phone with a bang.

"I know exactly who you are, son," the vice principal said. "Around here, students speak to staff, and especially me, only when spoken to. Let me see your records."

I handed them over. "Sure."

"Not one sport?" he said with a shake of his head. "I see you did get perfect attendance. I bet they gave you a shiny blue ribbon and everything back in Kentucky," he said, laying on the sarcasm.

Was it me, or did the vice principal have some kind of anger management issue? I let out a breath, trying not to take his attitude personally. I like to give everybody a second chance.

"You do well academically," he said with a snort. "What's your favorite subject?"

Since I had the encyclopedic power to telepathically access human knowledge, that was a tough call. I noticed Civil War books on a shelf behind his desk.

"*History,* sir," I said.

He turned and stared at the Civil War books on his shelf, then back at me with a who-do-you-think-you're-fooling look.

"What a coincidence," he said, letting my records drop to the desk.

I glanced out the window behind him. Under a pure

blue sky, palm trees were softly swaying in the seventy-two-degree Southern California breeze.

And I chose to attend school *why* again?

"Okay, history buff. I'll bump you into first-period Advanced Social Studies. The one I teach," he said, standing, as the bell rang.

Call me overly paranoid, but I wondered if maybe Mr. Marshman was somewhere on my List.

Chapter 20

SO THIS WAS HIGH SCHOOL—not too bad, not too good, could have been a lot more stimulating. I was coming out of bio lab, my last class of the day, when I brushed against a skinny freshman hurrying down the hall. He looked nervous and scared, and I felt kind of bad for the guy.

Then I heard his thoughts in my head. *Ugh. My sneakers are so six months ago. Everybody's checking out my shoes. Everybody's looking at me! Don't look at me. Please!*

I shook my head like a swimmer trying to get water out of his ears. I guess I was tired and my telepathic mental filters were shot. The *thoughts* of the students swirling around in the corridor were leaking into my head.

Well, well. Amanda's definitely flirting with me, I overheard a good-looking jock in a football jacket think as he winked at a pretty girl. *Back at you, baby.*

I quickened my pace, trying to get out of there. I can promise you that knowing everybody's secrets is nowhere near as cool as it sounds.

First day's over, and I haven't even talked to anybody, I suddenly heard in my head, and it wasn't my own voice. *I don't want to do this anymore. I hate this school.*

I stopped suddenly, looking around to see whose thoughts I'd just intercepted.

I spotted a tall, black-haired girl trying to lift a bulky backpack while also balancing a clarinet case. She turned around and I saw her face.

What felt like an invisible wall toppled over on me. She was really cute. Her eyes were amazing. So why was she so sad?

"Hi," I said, stepping in her direction. "Sorry to bother you. Uhmm, could you tell me where the library is?"

"No idea," she said quietly as she averted her eyes from mine. "I'm new here."

I shrugged. "So am I. Say, could I give you a hand with those books? I'm Daniel. Not that you asked."

She actually smiled, a half smile anyway. "I'm Phoebe

Cook," she said. Those eyes of hers were deep blue, flecked with silver. Gorgeous—and friendly. "So do you have a last name too, Daniel?"

I paused. Of course, I had a *fake* last name, but it never really feels like me somehow. It felt a little strange to say it to someone as genuine as Phoebe.

"Daniel Hopper."

"Nice to meet you, Daniel Hopper. I actually *could* use some help. Just to get my locker back open," Phoebe said. "Frankly, I don't know if I can lug all these books home."

I slid her bag off the floor and onto my shoulder.

"You're in luck," I said. "Lugging is one of my better talents."

She smiled again. "I thought you were looking for the library, Daniel."

She had me there. "I got a better offer, I guess."

"I guess you did. Well, let's see how you lug."

Chapter 21

I WALKED PHOEBE all the way home, and I enjoyed every second of it. She lived on South Cedar, about ten blocks from the high school. Her father was a computer salesman, and she told me they moved around a lot.

"Too much," said Phoebe with a wistful look that got to me. One of the really nice things about her—she was practically unconscious about how pretty she was. I completely understood her feeling about moving.

"My family moves a lot too," I said. "They're kind of free spirits." Definitely.

Daniel is gorgeous! I wonder if he would maybe ask me

out? she thought as we stopped in front of her house. *It's okay, Daniel. Go for it,* I heard Phoebe thinking. Wishing . . . encouraging.

I smiled, and felt a little light-headed, actually. News flash: I had never had a date with a human girl. So I'd never actually asked a girl out before. But Phoebe seemed so regular and nice, plus I'd just read her mind and she was interested in me. Still, I was afraid.

"Why don't we go to a movie, or maybe explore Glendale sometime?" I finally blurted out. Our hands grazed as I gave her back her bag.

"Okay," Phoebe said. "The movies, whatever. That'd be great. Good. You know what I mean."

She started up the stairs of her house, then stopped and turned back. Her blue eyes settled on me.

"Were you really looking for the library?" she asked.

I smiled. "Nope, I was looking for you."

"Good answer," she said, then disappeared inside.

And no, I didn't *create* Phoebe Cook, in case you're one of those people who like to look ahead in a story.

Chapter 22

I CAME THROUGH the front door of my rental house, checked everywhere for trouble, then collapsed on the couch. I knew high school was going to be a change of pace, maybe challenging, maybe anxiety producing, but I wasn't expecting boring—everything except Phoebe Cook, anyway.

After a while, I managed to peel myself up to start dinner. I didn't want to go too crazy, so I settled on a rosemary-crusted rack of lamb with truffle-spiked potato purée. As I cooked, I listened to a concerto by a classical guitarist named Rémi Boucher. The guy is not of this world, and I wondered if he was maybe another alien.

I've had the same thought about Tiger Woods, Bono, and, of course, Sanjaya Malakar.

After dinner I put on a fire and lay in front of it reading *Water for Elephants*. Ten minutes later, I put the book down, unable to concentrate the way I usually can.

I thought about Phoebe Cook.

I thought about Dana, my dream girlfriend.

Should I feel guilty? I didn't think so. I hadn't even kissed Phoebe. Yet.

I finally got up and made myself a pot of coffee. Then I cracked my knuckles and opened my laptop. The same one I'd found near the house where my parents were killed. Nothing better to get your mind off girls than thinking about aliens.

I brought up Ergent Seth's file and read it over again.

Alien: Ergent Seth, Number 6

Human Alias(es): ? Changes names on an as-needed basis, often hourly.

Area of Infestation: LA and Orange County, California. Central City, East la. Arizona. Nevada. Mexico. South and Central America. And still branching out.

Illegal Activities: Drug dealing, mass murder, abductions, torture, mind control and possession. Did we mention *mass murder?*

Planet of Origin: Gorto 4.
Alien Species: Vermgypian (see footnote).
Current Danger Level: Extremely high. Seth's goal is to de-populate Earth, then colonize it with his species. This violates every moral and ethical code extant.
Special Abilities: Telepathy, extraterrestrial Level 7 speed, Level 7 strength, shape-shifting, cunning, general viciousness.

The Level 7 strength concerned me. I was maybe a 3 on my best day. The slug in Portland had been a 4. I read the footnote next. Vermgypians were beyond strange. No one knew what they looked like beneath their demonic-appearing, armored containment suits. They were best known for the lethal nerve gas they emitted. If you were exposed, your cells started to melt. Then you rotted from the inside out. It was an extremely painful way to die.

Extremely.

Chapter 23

I LIKE THIS PLANET just the way it is, thank you very much—well, except for a few problems like poverty, war, polluted drinking water, and global warming—but I knew that Ergent Seth was on his way to making those crises seem like child's play.

It was time to check out la, and hopefully do some surveillance. In particular, I wanted to see the areas where Number 6 did his nastiest scut work, usually late at night.

"You sure you want me to drop you off *here,* mate?" the cabdriver said as we stopped at the corner of Sixth and San Pedro. Since I like to chat up a storm, I'd found out the cabby's name was Clive. He was a good-looking Brit who'd come to LA to—surprise, surprise—become a movie star.

"This part of town inn't fit for man nor beast after dark," Clive warned. "I'm not foolin'."

"I'll be all right," I told him. "This is where my job is. At Taco Bell. I'm a lettuce shredder. Love those chalupas."

I stood on the corner, probably looking a little lost, as the cab sped away. Truthfully, this part of LA seemed like a war zone with palm trees. Abandoned, deteriorating buildings and empty lots, plus a few single-occupancy hotels known as Homeless Hiltons. In the gutter at my feet, a rat was going to town inside a discarded Styrofoam tray from a local soup kitchen.

I stuck to the shadows as I did my recon. I was turning onto Towne Avenue when I saw a silver minivan pull to the curb. I figured it was a drug user looking to score. Then the doors slid open. Half a dozen kids between nine and twelve hopped out.

Isn't it a little late for a class trip? I thought, watching them shuffle across the street and strike a pose on the stairs of an abandoned factory.

"New stuff just in," I heard one of the younger ones call to a chrome-yellow Hummer passing by slowly. "China, china, burning white. Pure as the driven snow. Guaranteed to get you where you want to go."

I'd seen drug dealing before, in New York, London, even Portland. But I'd never seen such little kids dealing poison. *Who would use kids like this? Maybe Number 6?*

I hung back in a urine-scented doorway, watching as the kids did quick, hand-to-hand sales through car windows. What a disgrace. My blood was starting to boil.

About an hour later the silver van came around again. The driver-side door flew open.

A wiry, red-bearded skinhead in a brown leather jacket and a ponytail jumped out. Not Ergent Seth, my sixth sense told me, but maybe an important lackey of his. The kids rushed up to him, handing over money from their dealing. He restocked them with more plastic bags and vials.

I stared at the scene, fuming. Everything about the dealer was an abomination. Suddenly he backhanded a kid hard, knocking him onto the street, then went through his pockets for more money.

That was it, I thought, stepping out of the doorway. I couldn't take any more of this creepy, night-crawling, red-bearded vermin.

Chapter 24

"EXCUSE ME," I said as I approached the scuzzy dealer and felt my skin start to crawl. "Haven't I seen you on the tv show *Miami Ink*? No, my mistake. I think it was in the freak tent at the California State Fair. Or maybe Folsom Prison?"

The dealer smiled, showing off crooked, nicotine-stained teeth. Smiling was a good sign, I thought. Smiling meant he had already underestimated me.

"I'm looking for Ergent Seth," I told him. "You seen him around anywhere tonight?"

"Sounds to me like you're lookin' for Urgent Death."

And that was when the disgusting Dealer Man made his move.

I had to hand it to him. His dental hygiene left something to be desired, but he did have fast hands. The ice pick he stabbed at my throat traveled forward in a blur.

Fortunately I react pretty well to blurs.

I took a half step back, waited for him to overextend himself, then offered up a blur of my own—a roundhouse kick across the side of his head. The dealer flew back, his skinhead cracking into the van with a loud, dull *whump*.

He screeched and let go of the ice pick when I stepped down hard on the back of his hand. Then I kicked the weapon into the sewer.

"You ever heard of child labor laws?" I said.

He was going for a 9 millimeter automatic in his waistband when I had an inspiration.

I reached out suddenly and laid my hands on the sides of his head.

I stared into his eyes and unleashed a small fraction of my power of transformation.

For a moment the drug dealer writhed like somebody with the world's worst ice-cream headache. Then he tossed his gun into the sewer as if it burned his hand.

Next the red-bearded wonder climbed to the top of the abandoned factory stairs and thrust his arms out.

"*I . . . HAVE . . . BEEN . . . SAVED!*" the dealer screamed for all to hear.

The kids who worked for him stared with their mouths open wide.

"*I HAVE SEEN THE LIGHT!*" the dealer yelled even louder. "*AND I AM HERE IN THE NAME OF OUR LORD AND SAVIOUR TO MAKE SURE THAT EACH AND EVERY LAST ONE OF YOU SEES THAT SAME LIGHT!*"

I chuckled. In a way, he was right. I had definitely saved him. If you consider erasing his memory and convincing him that he was a Pentecostal preacher being saved.

The born-again dealer pointed at me as I backed away.

"You there! Yes, you! Like the Angel in Joseph's dream in the Holy Book, I say unto thee, *Do not be afraid!* Stay and hear the Good Word. For how else will you *save your soul from the clutches of the devil himself?*"

"I must be off now." I saluted him. "Maybe to do the Lord's work myself."

Hopefully, like catching Ergent Seth and dispatching him to the everlasting fires.

Chapter 25

WELCOME TO ANOTHER of my creepy nightmares. I kind of wish this were a blank page and I had nothing to say. But it isn't.

No sooner had I drifted off to sleep that night than Number 6 was talking to me, Ergent Seth himself. Imagine a dead and diseased horse's head on the body of a hairy, pasty white, six- or seven-hundred-pound wrestler. Now make it twice as ugly and scary. Oh yeah, and with horrifyingly bad breath.

"I have one word for you, Daniel—*run!* Because I have no plans of showing you the tender mercy The Prayer extended to your mama and papa.

"I will torture you for a human eternity, during which time you will *beg* me for death by an Opus 24/24, or an ax, or a thousand snakebites. I can see the future, Daniel, and I am looking forward to it, every excruciating second of your murder and dismemberment. Isn't that a wonderful English word, *dis-member-ment?*

"Now, *wake up, dear boy*—and enjoy another sleepless night, compliments of Ergent Seth."

Chapter 26

SLEEP-DEPRIVED OR NOT, I forced myself to go to school the next day. Got to keep those priorities straight. It's amazing how *not* having parents makes you be a parent to yourself. Most of the time, anyway.

Two things happened when I was coming out of my last class. Two awesomely cool things, actually.

"There you are," Phoebe Cook said, smiling as she jogged over. "I've been looking everywhere for you, Daniel."

Then she actually hooked my arm with hers, and I could feel pins and needles on the inside of my elbow where our skin touched. If it was a question before, it was now confirmed. I definitely had a bit of a crush on Phoebe. Dana wasn't going to like this, but I couldn't help what was happening. *Sorry, Dana.*

"How about that movie? Maybe Friday?" I said as we walked. I think I was blushing. "Am I being too pushy?"

This Friday? Yes! I heard Phoebe thinking. *No, wait. Maybe I shouldn't seem too eager to go out with Daniel. He might get the wrong idea.*

"Um, can I let you know?" Phoebe said. "I might have to babysit at home."

"Sure," I said, not wanting Phoebe to feel the least bit uncomfortable. "No worries."

We stopped in the front of my house, and Phoebe suddenly pointed over my shoulder.

"Awww! How cute," she said, and smiled sweetly. *Yep, I definitely had a crush on her.* "What's your cat's name?" she asked.

I turned and saw a large tabby standing on the sill of my open kitchen window. My jaw and stomach dropped simultaneously.

Not only *didn't* I have a cat—security nut that I am—I had made triple sure to lock all the windows.

"Crap," I said.

"That's a funny name for a cat," Phoebe said, and rolled her eyes.

"Isn't it?" I mumbled, hustling up my front porch steps. "I have to go, Phoebe. I'll see you tomorrow. Gotta feed the cat."

Or maybe get eaten by it.

Chapter 27

THE FRONT DOOR CREAKED OPEN by itself *trés* creepily when I touched the knob.

I stopped in the doorway and did a quick mental scan of the house to see if there was someone or some*thing* still inside. I didn't sense anything—so I stepped all the way in.

First thing I noticed was the ripped-apart couch cushions in the living room. *Crap!* Next was the waterfall rushing down the stairs. *Double crap!* I could hear an open tap in the upstairs bathroom, probably the bathtub.

While I was assessing the water damage, I noticed

burnt-rubber tire marks across the floor, as if someone had ridden a motorcycle through the house. I think someone had.

"There goes the security deposit," I mumbled, nimbly stepping around my new indoor wading pool.

Next I noticed something smoldering in the fireplace. It was my book *Water for Elephants*. What kind of thoughtless creep would burn a book?

The kitchen had taken the worst of the attack. It looked like someone had removed everything from the fridge, item by item, and smashed the bottles and cartons against the wall. The alley cat that I'd seen in the shattered window was standing on the counter now, licking up spilt milk.

"Oh, there you are," I said. *"Crap."*

There was another cat on the floor, a cute calico that rubbed its cheek against my shin as it purred.

"What happened here?" I mumbled. Suddenly Tabby leaped off the counter and attached itself to my face.

I backpedaled, screaming as it hooked several claws into my lower lip and bit into my cheek. The smaller cat attacked too, wrapping itself around my leg like a python with claws, and sinking its teeth deep into my shin. I flicked off the kitten first, sending it through the air, then sliding across the counter and into a wall.

There was a hideous Velcro-like rip of skin as I

detached the tabby from my face and hurled it away.

It hissed at me angrily, looking at me with strangely human eyes.

"Get out of LA or die!" it croaked in a demonic voice.

Before I could react, it hopped onto the counter and the two cats disappeared out the kitchen window. "We'll be back . . . *mouse-boy!*" they said in chorus.

Chapter 28

WITHOUT YOUR FRIENDS, well, what are you?

Willy, Joe, Emma, and Dana were only too happy to help me clean up after the crazy cat attack. Dana seemed a little distant, like maybe she knew about Phoebe Cook. She didn't say much, though, as she tended to the bloody patch of raw flesh on my face.

I looked at myself in the mirror. "Great. I look like I just stepped out of a B horror movie with a very bad make-up job."

"Why should you care what you look like?" Dana said without smiling, not expecting an answer. That was my first sign that she wasn't too pleased about Phoebe.

Afterward I treated everyone to pizza, but I made the mistake of letting Joe order.

"No, not one *with* everything," I heard him tell the phone person at Domino's. "One *of* everything. I'd like the entire menu. In fact, make it two entire menus."

"Domino's?" Emma said in shock. "If you want to kill yourself, fine, but I don't do processed flour. Hello? This is California. There has to be a Whole Foods around here somewhere."

She was already searching the Yellow Pages when the phone rang. I figured it was the pizza place, confirming Joe's insane order.

"Hello?" I said.

"Hello, indeed," a cultured voice said.

It was Seth. Don't ask me how I knew for sure, I just did. Just like I knew he was the one who'd trashed my place with his crazy felines.

"Who's this?" I said, playing dumb.

"Who's *this?*" the voice repeated almost sorrowfully. "Now is that remotely proper etiquette? Wouldn't 'May I help you?' be a tad more polite? Bad enough they send a boy for me, but a crude American one with no manners? Nonetheless, to answer your impolite question, I think you know who I am. Though I daresay, if you don't follow my advice very, very soon, you're going to wish you did not."

"Um, sorry?" I said, still stunned. I'd never spoken to a gas before, let alone one that sounded like it had trained with the Royal Shakespeare Company. "I really think you have the wrong number."

"Better the wrong number," the confident British voice said, "than the wrong city, Daniel. By the way, I heard you had a little problem today—with kitty cats. Or should I say *kitty litter?*"

Panic rose at the mention of my name. And the cats.

Ergent Seth not only knew where I was, he knew *who* I was!

Chapter 29

"OH, YES," Seth leisurely continued. "I know who you are, Dan. In fact, I've been patiently waiting for you ever since that unfortunate accident with that silly Arbilitorarian pretender in the sewers of Portland.

"Perhaps you are under the impression that there is some similar business to take care of between you and me. But there is not. Because of your youth, I am paying you this final courtesy. You can't say I didn't give you fair warning. First the dream. Then the visit from my feline friends. Now an actual phone call.

"Move on! Skip me and go on to the next on your *List,*

if that is your foolish desire. To each his own, or, as my American friends so charmingly say, it's a free country. But if you value your life, then you do not wish to meet with me, little boy—for I am death its very self. *Nothing* that has ever encountered me has lived to tell the tale."

Seth was more like a *gasbag* than a gas, I thought. He sure seemed to love the sound of his own voice. Too bad I didn't.

"Okay. That's interesting. But my name's not Daniel, and I have no idea what you're talking about," I said, still playing dumb. "You have a good day."

I hung up on him.

Then I nearly jumped out of my skin as the phone rang again.

I bent down immediately and ripped the cord out of the wall.

But as I stood there, something happened that shook my confidence a little. The phone, with its tattered cord dangling beside it, rang again.

Cold beads of sweat were rolling down my spinal column. My heart was pounding.

The answering machine beside the phone picked up after the second ring. *Was that even possible?*

"Dan? Hello? I do believe we've become disconnected," the clipped British voice said from the speaker. "Never say I didn't give you a chance, dear boy. The kid gloves are now officially off. You are now Dead Boy Walking."

Seth began to chuckle softly. The chuckle morphed into a bloodcurdling kind of clicking sound. Like a cricket, a thousand-pound one.

All of a sudden, my lungs and face were burning. Then I started gagging. I opened my mouth to tell my friends that I was choking, but nothing came out. I fell to my knees.

That's when Willy dove to the floor. He lifted the answering machine by its cord and smashed it to pieces.

My breath returned in a sweet, life-preserving rush.

"Seth isn't your regular, garden-variety slimer, is he?" Willy said.

"I'm beginning to think," I said between greedy gulps of air, "maybe not."

At this I heard a horrifying noise outside. Cats! Hundreds of them, shrieking in the night, calling out my name.

They knew who I was too.

Chapter 30

I GOT TO SCHOOL EARLY the next day. Why school? Maybe because I'd learned my lesson in Portland. Or maybe it was because Phoebe Cook would be there. Honestly? I'd say five percent the lesson in Portland, ninety-five percent Phoebe.

My first class was history with Mr. Marshman, and he was right on time, looking sappier and happier than I'd ever seen him. Why was he so giddy and joyful?

"Pop quiz time!" he announced.

I noticed how I was the only one in the class who didn't groan like it was the end of the world. Look on the bright side, I wanted to tell them as I took the handout. At least we're not all on the floor sucking alien nerve gas and incapable of breathing.

Yet.

And fortunately, the quiz wasn't all that hard.

What are the names of the two oldest, most complete hominid skeletons? *Duh, Lucy and Little Foot, maybe.* What was the first known great civilization? *Depends on your point of view,* I thought, mentally flipping through the origin dates of thousands of major alien tribes, some who made it to Earth long before anything in our history textbook. But I wrote the answer Marshman wanted: *The Sumerians.* These people had no idea . . .

I was breezing along okay when I suddenly dropped my pen. Hold up! It wasn't too smart for me to show off, was it? I erased what I'd written so far and started scribbling wrong answers one after the other.

I handed my test in first, and Marshman graded it in about half a minute flat.

"Wow!" he exclaimed. "Just to let everyone know, Linus and Cujo were not the oldest hominid skeletons. Las Vegas is not the first known great civilization, and Sauron was not the Babylonian king who kept the Jews in captivity. Daniel, I really want to thank you. You've provided a perfect example of what *not* to do in my class."

I felt my face flush as everyone in the room laughed at

me. I kept my head down as I walked up and got my test. A big red *0* was written across the top, which actually kind of hurt my feelings.

Ground control to Daniel, I thought. *Maybe you're playing this dumb game a little too well.*

Chapter 31

"STEP BACK, EVERYBODY. Give him room. Here comes Albert Daniel Einstein," some wise guy said as I came out of history class.

One of the school tough guys was talking to his buddies in the hall. I was trying to walk around him when he grabbed my shirt and shoved me hard against a locker.

"Guys, feast your eyes on Daniel Hopper, the mindless new kid. Stand back! I speak brain-dead."

"*Me* Jake," another kid said, patting his Abercrombie & Fitch polo shirt. He poked me hard in the chest with his finger. "*You* halfwit."

My instinct was to deal with bullies the way all pathetic, attention-seeking, disturbed individuals need to be dealt with—by ignoring them. But I was on edge that morning, and he was picking at a nerve.

I stared at his index finger, debating whether I should snap it at the first knuckle or the second.

A janitor's mop bucket across the hall solved my dilemma. At a speed approximating that of sound, I shot my left leg behind Jake's and shoved the six-foot, two-hundred-something-pounder with my right palm. He actually went airborne before he landed, butt down, in the slop bucket.

"Watch those wet floors, and have a super day," I said before I disappeared around the corner.

Only to barely avoid a head-on collision with Phoebe Cook coming out the door of the bio lab. She looked incredible again today.

"I was hoping to bump into you, Daniel," Phoebe said. "Well, not literally, I guess, but do you have a free period now? I was wondering if we could talk. Please?"

I actually had geometry class, but why bring up pesky details? "Of course," I said. "I finally figured out where the library is."

Which made her laugh.

Which made me kind of goofily happy.

Chapter 32

PHOEBE AND I SAT on a couple of footstools in a far
corner of the library stacks. Our knees were almost
touching, and mine were knocking a little. No one else
was anywhere around.

For about a minute, she stayed there staring at me
while she gnawed on her lower lip. Then her eyes welled
up with tears.

"What is it?" I whispered.

"I can't fake it anymore," Phoebe said in a shaky voice.
"I lied to you about my dad moving us because of his job.
We relocated because something awful, really awful,

happened to our family.

"Last July, my little sister, Allison, went out to chalk on the driveway after swimming lessons and . . . she never came back. She was abducted. Somebody took her, Daniel. She was six years old. She'd be seven now."

I sat there stunned into silence. I hadn't known what Phoebe was going to say, but I definitely wasn't expecting this kind of revelation.

Phoebe started to sob. She balled her fists in my shirt, and I could feel her shuddering against my chest.

"I'm sorry," I finally managed. "I'm so sorry, Phoebe."

As I wiped away her tears, I felt the worst kind of sadness inside myself. This was what was so different about Phoebe, I realized. It was our connection. *We'd both lost people, people we'd loved.*

"I know what you're feeling," I said. "I lost a sister too."

Her name was Pork Chop.

Chapter 33

I LEFT PHOEBE at the doorway of her next class and immediately headed for the nearest exit. I was too wired to be in school right now. I needed to figure some things out. Maybe her sister's disappearance wasn't a coincidence. According to The List, Ergent Seth abducted kids. Was it possible that he had Allison? Of course it was. Keep this in mind: *there are no coincidences.*

I was coming across the teachers' parking lot when I heard a low, whooshing sound, like a bottle rocket or something. The side window of the bmw in front of me vaporized in a shower of flying glass.

There were two more barely audible whooshes as I flipped and somersaulted along the asphalt between two parked cars, trying not to be hit. A couple of deep gouges blew out of the concrete where my head had been.

So this is what Seth meant when he said the gloves were off.

I poked my head up and spotted a muzzle flash at the top of the football equipment shed. Another projectile zipped past my ear, close enough for me to hear the air pop. This craziness had to stop right now, before somebody got hurt. The problem was that a whole football field stood between me and the enemy with a rocket launcher.

I closed my eyes and concentrated hard. When I opened them again, Willy was crouched there beside me.

"Whoa! What's going on, dude?" he said. "I was sleepin' in, y'know?"

"I'm getting shot at. The shells are about the size of bowling balls."

"Cool!" Willy said.

"*Not* cool," I said.

He glanced at the car we were crouched behind. A third-generation Chevy Cavalier. "This will do," he said. Then Willy punched a hole in the window. He yanked open the driver's door. "I'm in. Nice interior."

He kicked at the steering column until he cracked the plastic.

"Damn! Ignition wires are supposed to be red. This looks like colored spaghetti. Daniel—color of ignition wires for a '97 Chevy Cavalier?"

I went through pictures and pages of the car manual—yes, *in my head,* there's lots stored in there, trust me—till I found what I was looking for.

"Pink!" I said.

"MacGyver, eat your heart out!" Willy giggled, then yanked the two pink wires out. He touched their sparking ends together. There was a chug-chugging sound and then the engine turned over.

"Willy, you kick butt," I said, and crawled into the driver's seat. I ripped the transmission into reverse, then pounded down on the accelerator.

Last but not least, I disappeared Willy again. "Thanks, dude! Catch you later."

I hope.

Chapter 34

THE CAVALIER'S BACK WINDSHIELD got blown away as I gunned it through the chain-link fence of the football field. *No*, I don't have a license in any state. *Yes*, I'm a pretty good driver anyway.

My fiendish opponent wised up when I was at the ten-yard line and closing on him. Talk about a touchdown dance! I flattened the uprights before I hit the corrugated steel equipment shed at about fifty.

It sounded like a bomb had gone off on the athletic field. The air was filled with shoulder pads and tackling dummies and helmets sporting big blue *G*'s for Glendale.

I threw the Cavalier into park and jumped out just as the sniper landed loudly on the car's hood.

The first thing I noticed was his gun. It was definitely an off-world weapon, a notorious Opus 24/24. The kind of gun that killed my mom and dad. I *really* didn't like them, so I snapped it in half over my knee.

The gunman was moaning as I picked him up over my head.

"You. Are. Toast. Unless you tell me where Seth—" I started to say as a steel chain swung around my throat. *Alien-hunting lesson number thirty-seven,* I thought. *Save the wisecracks until you're sure your opponent is working alone.*

This really muscular walking tattoo parlor was trying to strangle me. I gave the gunman a heave and rammed myself and, more important, Mr. Muscles back against the remaining equipment shed wall. Once! Twice! But the third time was the charm. Now he was out for the count too.

I dragged the two of them together and placed my hands on their heads. *What to do, what to do?* I took a deep, centering breath, and all my *power* was there.

There was nothing, *nothing* like the feeling. Think of the best you've ever felt physically, lying down after a long run, dropping yourself into a favorite chair after a long day at school, plunging into a pool on a hot day.

111

Now, times it by a million or so.

My power was everything good and bright and alive absorbed and condensed into pure energy. I was its portal. I felt it bubble up like molten metal from my chest, through my arms, into my hands.

"I now pronounce you . . . elephant turds," I told my attackers. "And yes, I'm serious about that."

Both morons curled into fetal positions. They lay on the grass with their eyes open, limp and motionless. Like, well, elephant turds.

How do you like that? My mighty mastodon obsession had finally paid off big-time. Maybe my friends wouldn't be teasing me about it anymore.

By the way, I'm not crazy for thinking elephants are completely amazing. You will too when you know this true story: Elephants were brought to Earth about three million years ago. *From my planet.* It was my people's gift to Terra Firma.

How's that for an FYI?

Elephants are aliens too!

Chapter 35

I HURRIED HOME and took two emergency reconnaissance jogs around the house. Everything seemed okay, but I came in through the backyard anyway. Just in case another Seth killer or two were watching my front door.

I almost snapped my key off in the lock when the door suddenly opened.

I jumped back, zigzagging, and dove behind an elm tree, waiting for Opus Magnum gunfire.

What came instead was soft laughter and the unmistakable smell of bacon. I peeked very carefully around the side of the tree trunk.

"Mom?"

She stood in the open doorway, wiping her hands on the homiest flowered apron you might see in the entire state of Kansas.

"There you are, Daniel," she said. "How would you like your eggs, sweetie?"

What? I thought, following her inside. How could Mom appear when I hadn't actively created her? That hadn't happened before. Suddenly I was a little nervous that maybe Seth was controlling my mind—and her. He'd already shown me what he could do through the telephone.

I decided I better do a little security check here, but if this *wasn't* my mom, I knew I'd start screaming. "What's Dad's name?" I asked.

She tilted her head my way. "Graff. Sometimes it's Harold Hopper. One time it was Robert Zimmerman. Do I pass?"

"You pass, Mom."

A plate was set for me on the kitchen island. It was piled high: bacon, on top of eggs, on top of hash browns, on top of pancakes. I could feel my mouth water as my mom poured warm maple syrup all over everything.

Breakfast in the afternoon was definitely breakfast my way!

Chapter 36

HEY, WHO CARES how she got here? I decided as I clutched a knife and fork and dug in.

Besides, these were definitely my mom's pancakes—no one else could whip 'em up like her—not even Seth, I was certain.

"What's that all about?" my mom said as I mopped up the last bit of syrup. She was referring to my ripped-up face plus the recent addition of a large, jagged cut on my elbow.

"This little scratch? This little *nothing?* C'mon. I'm an Alien Hunter."

She wasn't having any of it. "Okay, upstairs. March!" she said. "Hut, one, two . . ."

I sat on the edge of the bathtub with my eyes closed as she peroxided and bacitracined and bandaged my arm. I finally told her what was going on. The news about Phoebe's sister. The attack in the school parking lot. How I'd gotten away.

She shook her head. "Elephant turds? Daniel, that is completely beneath you."

I stared at her with an exaggerated expression of outrage—until she finally grinned. "Okay, okay. Beneath you *and* more than a little funny," she said, ruffling my hair. "You and your elephants."

Finally I had to ask Mom if she knew how she'd gotten into the house without my help.

She shook her head. "Maybe your subconscious called me. Perhaps you're worried, Daniel, as you should be. I pray that you're ready for Number 6, son."

I looked into her eyes. "Mom, who do you pray to?"

"I just pray, Daniel. That's all."

Chapter 37

PHOEBE HAD CALLED me on my cell and asked to meet at the coffee place on South Brand Boulevard a couple of ticks past three. I waved her over to the club chairs I'd snagged next to the fireplace. Be still, my heart.

"First off, I want to apologize," Phoebe said, putting down her bag. "I totally lost it with you this morning. It isn't fair for me to dump my family troubles on you. Forget I said anything, okay? I . . ."

I took Phoebe's hand and squeezed gently as I stared into her blue eyes. My mouth was going dry again. Was that because I wanted to kiss her more than anything I'd ever wanted before?

"Look," I said. "I wouldn't stop helping if you told me to. We're going to find your sister. Somehow."

She squeezed back, a sign of thanks. Then she produced a manila folder from her bag and dropped it on the table.

"That's the police file on my sister's case. My folks don't know I have it."

I read through Allison's missing persons file in a couple of seconds. There had been no witnesses. No sign of suspicious vehicles. No nothing.

Allison had gone out to play at around one in the afternoon. When her mother checked on her, she was simply and inexplicably gone. And she had not been heard from again.

My instincts told me that it had something to do with Seth. Did I mention there's an active slave market for human children? Every single day kids are lifted off this planet. That's the truth. They're used for labor, and by some alien species—*hurl alert*—as pets.

I wanted to tell Phoebe what I knew, but I couldn't get the words out. Besides, I had no urge to sound completely demented and deranged.

On the last page of the police file was a list of names and addresses. Someone had typed "Potential Pattern" and

"Awaiting GP" across its top. For the next twenty minutes or so, we Googled the names on Phoebe's laptop through the coffee shop's Wi-Fi.

There was a pattern at least. The kids had been taken mostly from Simi Valley, Beverly Hills, and Culver City. The abductions made an almost perfect connect-the-dots circle with Malibu at its direct center.

Malibu, I thought. Where Seth was supposed to live. Was that where Phoebe's sister was now?

Malibu? I thought, finishing my coffee.

The outer reaches of the Andromeda galaxy?

Either-or.

Chapter 38

I GAVE PHOEBE a kind of brotherly hug before she stood to leave. I wanted to try to comfort her and, what the heck, just, you know, hug her. I couldn't believe how good she smelled. Her hair, everything. Like a garden I'd visited once in the French countryside. Yep, that good.

"We're going to find Allison," I whispered before she broke away. "I promise, Phoebe."

As I watched her leave, I tried to convince myself that I actually would find her sister, rescue her from *whatever*, and bring her back safely to the Cook family.

I can do that, I thought to myself. *Or I don't deserve to have The List, do I.*

Outside the coffee shop, it was California perfect. Room temperature, no wind, a tangerine sunset in the cloudless sky. As I walked home, I hoped Phoebe's sister was still around to see it.

I was lost in deep thought when I reached out to open the wrought iron gate in front of my house.

Hey, wait a second! Hold up! This house doesn't have a wrought iron gate!

I double-checked the address. There was no mistake. I couldn't believe it.

My house wasn't there anymore!

I stood and stared at rows of headstones, stone angels, weather-beaten tilted crosses. Worse, I could smell the rotting dead all around me.

It was Seth! He'd turned my house into a cemetery.

Not a cutesy, grammar-school, Halloween-decorated-gym kind of cemetery either. We're talking a heart-bursting, run-for-your-life, *Night of the Living Dead*-style boneyard.

The worst of it was a Greek temple-sized granite mausoleum with *Daniel* carved above Doric columns. Just in case I didn't get the message. Seth was off-the-chart powerful.

I looked up and down the street to see if any of my

neighbors were walking around. The place seemed deserted. How long had the house been a graveyard? I needed to change it back, but how? I'd transformed things before, but I'd never reversed somebody else's trans-formation. Could I actually do that? I had no idea.

Only one way to find out. I cleared my head and closed my eyes. Then I pictured the rental property the way it used to look, in extremely vivid and precise detail. I concentrated on the image from the past.

Seconds later, I popped open my eyes.

I winced and groaned out loud. The cemetery was gone, but the building I'd created was a replica of the one I'd lived in when I was in Portland. Worse, the two cops from the Runaway Juvenile Unit were standing on the porch. They called out, "Daniel! C'mere, Daniel! We want to talk to you, buddy. Where's your crazy mom and dad?"

I clamped my eyes shut, concentrated, and tried again. Very slowly, I opened my eyes.

Yes! *It had worked.* The house was back to normal, at least it looked that way. Just a little reorganization of atoms and molecules, that's all.

I immediately turned around and left the way I'd come. My home base was officially compromised.

Much worse, *I* was officially compromised.

Chapter 39

BASICALLY, I WENT INTO HIDING for the rest of the day. Hiding *and* worrying.

When it was dark, I cut through a lot of backyards until I got to Phoebe's house.

I wanted to talk to her about her sister and a few other monumentally troubling things, but mostly I just felt comfortable around Phoebe. She was my first human friend.

I stopped myself as I was about to ring her front doorbell. Hold up! It was past eleven at night. How was this going to work? *Oh, hi, Mr. or Mrs. Cook. I'm Daniel, your daughter's alien friend. Could I talk to her a sec?*

I was trying to figure out something clever when I saw a light blink on in an upstairs bedroom toward the rear of the house. Then I caught a quick glimpse of Phoebe. So I jogged along the hedge-lined driveway.

I was down on my knees, searching for something to toss up at the window, when I heard a growl at the back of my neck. *Not good! Not a sound I like to hear.*

I turned and was suddenly face to jowl with somebody's angry Rottweiler.

Emma, I thought, and concentrated fiercely. *Emma! Help! Right this instant!*

And there she was in all her glory. "Hey, Daniel," Emma said, flipping a French braid over her shoulder. "What's up?"

"Hello?" I whispered, pointing at the monstrous dog. "Dog! Teeth! Froth on chin!"

Emma immediately wrapped the massive thing in a playful headlock, making it coo like a newborn as she scratched under its sharklike jaw.

"This cutie?" she asked, wiping away the drool with her finger, then flicking it at me.

"You rule, Emma," I said as I backed away from her and the Rot. "I owe you one."

"I owe *you.* Thanks for thinking me here. I just love doggies."

Chapter 40

FOR THE NEXT half minute or so, I searched for something to get me up to the brightly lit second-story window without alerting Phoebe's parents. The best I could find was a backyard trampoline. A quick test bounce showed that it wasn't quite the catapult I was looking for.

I scampered up onto the roof of the toolshed. From there I jumped onto the trampoline and actually made it to the half-porch on the second floor. Phoebe was at her laptop behind an open window. When she saw me, she nearly fell out of her swivel chair.

"Daniel? Is that you? What are you doing here?"

"Sorry. I wasn't sure if it was cool to ring the doorbell this late. I got into a major blowout with my parents. I didn't know where else to go," I sputtered. "I should just leave, right?"

"No, it's okay, I guess," Phoebe said, still looking puzzled, and who could blame her? "Just be really, really quiet. And hey—it's nice to see you. I was thinking about you before."

"Anything new on Allison?" I asked once I was safely inside her room.

"Nothing," Phoebe said, and shook her head sadly. "But I'm glad you're here. I was thinking that maybe we could skip school and go to Malibu tomorrow. To look for Allison."

Chapter 41

GO TO THE BEACH with Phoebe instead of school? I thought. *I could certainly handle that.*

A few minutes later Phoebe took down a chess set from her shelf, and for the next hour, we gorged ourselves on microwave popcorn and played. Phoebe was really good. I've played ibm's Deep Blue program, so I'm a pretty fair judge of talent.

"I thought you said you only played a little," I said as she took my second knight. "I think I'm being hustled. You think I wouldn't notice that totally obscure Konstanti-nopolsky opening? Who taught you that? Kasparov?"

"Hey, I told you I was a closet geek," she said, smiling. Which was weird, because when I looked up about two seconds later, a tear was running down Phoebe's cheek.

"Hey, don't do that. Aren't you supposed to cry if you're *losing?*"

"It's not that," Phoebe said, wiping her eyes. "I'm actually happy. Can't you tell?"

"And that's why you're crying?"

"It's just . . . I was so bummed out that first day of school, and then I turned around and there you were. Now you're trying to help me find Allison. It's like fate or something, you know, Daniel? You're like my guardian angel. I don't mean to be corny, but—"

"Phoebe?" a man's voice called from the hall. "Are you still awake? C'mon, sweetheart. Lights out. You have school in the morning."

I was at the window, about to dive for the bushes, when Phoebe grabbed me. And held me against her body, which was kind of nice, I must say.

"It's okay, Daniel. He's gone. Let me fix a place for you to sleep."

I stood there watching Phoebe arrange pillows and sheets. *She isn't thinking that I . . . I mean, she doesn't think that she and I would . . . what?*

A pillow hit me square in the face.

"You sleep in the closet here, Daniel. In case my mom

or dad opens the door, okay? See you in the morning."

"Oh yeah. The closet. Perfect," I said.

"Night, Daniel," said Phoebe.

"Night, Phoebe," I said.

From the closet.

Not so terrible, actually.

Safe anyway.

Chapter 42

MY DREAMS that night were as vivid as ever, six hours of full 1080p resolution. Which would have been really great if every dream hadn't been a *soul-sucking, bloodcurdling nightmare that no one in their right mind would watch after dark.*

In the worst one, The Prayer was chasing me through my house with a couple of bloody scythes. As I ran into the kitchen, the floor gave way under my feet, and I fell face-first through a moldering coffin onto the chest of a decomposed corpse in a wedding dress. I stared into empty eye sockets as peeling, blackened lips pursed themselves together, ready to give me a kiss. The corpse was Phoebe!

Shoe boxes in the closet went flying as I woke up, flailing. I wiped my sweat-drenched face with a sleeve before I poked my head out the closet door.

Phoebe wasn't in her bed. That was funny. Funny odd. The room was dark. The alarm clock on the desk said it was 6:51. Had she gotten up already?

I listened for the sound of a shower.

Nothing.

The alarm clock clicked to 6:52 as I glanced over at the open window above her unmade bed. A bad feeling started in the pit of my stomach. This was weird. *Where was she?*

I pulled on my sneakers and decided to search the house for Phoebe, forgetting that her parents might see me. At alien hyperspeed, I blurred through the upper three bedrooms.

Phoebe wasn't in the shower.

Phoebe wasn't anywhere in the bedrooms.

Not in the attic either.

Phoebe was gone.

Chapter 43

I STOPPED OUTSIDE the kitchen doorway when I heard her parents talking in there.

"What do you mean she's not in the house?" Phoebe's mom was saying.

"I noticed her school bag's gone," her dad said. "Maybe she went in early to study. I'm sure there's a perfectly reasonable explanation."

I heard a phone lift.

"Who are you calling?" asked Phoebe's father.

"The police," said her mom.

"Honey, there's no need to panic. We should think this through."

"She's the only daughter we have left," her mom said, sounding as freaked as I was feeling. "You *think* it through while I *do* something."

No, I thought, closing my eyes. *This is not good.* People just didn't disappear in the middle of the night. At least not willingly. If Phoebe wanted to head to Malibu without me, she would have said something. I was right there in the closet, wasn't I?

I fast-forwarded myself down the hallway, through the family room, and out the front door.

I had to find Phoebe.

Before Ergent Seth did.

Chapter 44

MY PANIC STATE had pretty much quadrupled by the time I burst through Glendale High's front doors a few minutes later. I raced up and down the halls, ripping open doors and sticking my head into empty classrooms like a lunatic escaped from an alien asylum.

There goes her dad's theory, I thought, sprinting through the deserted cafeteria. *Phoebe isn't here at school.* Not even in the corner of the library where she'd first told me about her sister's being missing.

Phoebe's words from the night before burned in my ears as I passed her locker.

You're like my guardian angel.

Yeah, I thought, sick with worry. *Or maybe I'm the one who led Seth to you.*

"There you are," Mr. Marshman said as he practically clotheslined me in front of his office. "We've been trying to call your house. There was a mix-up, and we forgot to give you your placement exam. I'm glad you're here early. You can take the test now. This is perfect."

Was this guy kidding me? Like I needed a test now? Like I didn't have enough on my mind already?

I let out a deep breath as I glanced over his shoulder at the nearest exit. Should I just bolt? Phoebe obviously wasn't here. Maybe she'd headed to Malibu on her own. Or maybe Seth had taken her to keep her sister company?

"Mr. Marshman, with all due respect, I really can't do this now," I said.

"I think you can, Mr. Hopper." He handed me a booklet and pencil. "I *know* you can, Mr. Hopper."

"All right, fine." I practically ripped the test out of his hands. I leaned it against the nearest wall, speed-read my way through it, marking off answer after answer with machine-gun rapidity.

Maybe thirty seconds later, forty tops, I broke the pencil in half on the last of the one hundred multiple-choice fill-ins. I shoved the test into Marshman's face.

"Don't bother to grade it. I aced it," I said, taking a step for the exit. "Now, I have to go! Every once in a while something is actually more important than school! Hard to believe, I know!"

Marshman suddenly made a grunting sound and shifted like a linebacker to his left, blocking my path.

"I knew you were trouble the first time I laid eyes on you," he said, red-faced. "My instincts are never wrong, Hopper."

That's it. Enough of this nonsense, I thought.

Up and down the school hallway, I levitated all the student lockers. Then I levitated Mr. Marshman until his bullet head touched the ceiling and he yelped with surprise and disbelief.

"How—how did you do that?"

"You don't want to know," I said, gazing into his astounded eyes. "Now you stay right there—for thirty minutes. Let's call it a time-out!"

Then I left school—in a *blur*.

Chapter 45

I BURST OUT the back exit into the parking lot.

First I scanned all the cars.

Then the athletic fields. Beyond the wrecked equipment shed, a team was starting early soccer practice.

Maybe Phoebe had joined the soccer team, I thought. No, that didn't make sense. *You're losing it, Daniel. This isn't like you.*

I picked up my pace when I saw that one of the girls near the far goal had long black hair. Phoebe? The soccer coach blew her whistle as I ran past.

I was about midfield when the dark-haired girl finally

turned around. My heart sank. Unless Phoebe had suddenly turned Asian American, I was in the wrong place at the wrong time.

"What do you think you're doing?" the coach yelled, charging toward me.

I wish I knew.

Then I heard a girl scream, and I recognized the voice immediately.

"Phoebe!" I yelled, my eyes burning as I half-ran, half-clawed my way up a steep slope beyond the athletic fields. "I'm coming . . . Hold on!"

I finally broke the top of the rise a second later. Thank the heavens, Phoebe was there. She was in a clearing, down on her knees, crying. I wasn't too late! I'd found her. I ran up and wrapped her in my arms, feeling the familiar warmth of her body.

"Oh Daniel, something really horrible," she whispered, trembling, "something unspeakable, is about to happen. I just know it. I'm sure of it."

Chapter 46

"IT'S OKAY, PHOEBE," I said as I rocked her gently back and forth. "I'm here now. Everything is okay. It's my fault. I'm so sorry. I'm so sorry."

"You can say that again," Phoebe said, suddenly stiffening in my arms.

What the—?

She squirmed away. Then Phoebe gave me a funny smile. Not funny ha-ha. Funny *weird*. Funny *contemptuous*. Funny *sickening*.

"What?" I said. "Phoebe? Are you okay? What's going on here?"

"You are so dumb, it's amazing," she said, shaking her head. "You still haven't figured it out."

"Figured what out?" I said warily.

Suddenly I fell back, blinded, as a silver-tinged explosion flashed before my eyes. Where Phoebe's sneakers had been, there was now a huge pair of men's black shoes. I slowly panned up—long black trousers, a black silk shirt, kinky chin whiskers.

"Wh-wh-wh-what?" I said. Something very articulate and meaningful like that.

Above the collar of the black shirt was an impossibly narrow, horselike head, a *dead* horse's head, covered in slack, bone-white, bloodless skin. The skin was decorated with pea-sized, pusoozing bumps, like a diseased chicken's.

I stared into the monster's eyes. Shiny, bulging, blood-red orbs embedded in the loose skin like larvae.

"Ironic, isn't it? Here you were, knocking yourself out to find me." A voice came from a rattling flap and a hole below the demonic eyes. A British voice. *Seth's* voice.

He switched back into Phoebe—and batted those startling blue eyes at me.

"And here I was the whole time," came Seth's voice—*out of Phoebe's mouth.*

Chapter 47

"WAIT A SECOND," I said, trying to stop the sudden, awful spinning in my head. "That means . . . all along you were . . . Right from the start you were . . ."

Seth changed himself from Phoebe back into the horse-headed monster—that is, *himself*.

"Phoebe? Oh yes," he said, winking an orb as the corners of his mouth pulled up in a horsey smile. "You're quite a snuggler, Danny. I'll always cherish the time we had."

I closed my eyes and slowly shook my head. Talk about something sucking big-time. I'd been getting all googly-eyed and fog-brained over an alien slime pustule. Wow. I'd wanted to die before, but never so badly. I probably would in a second anyway. Cardiac arrest by embarrassment.

"Quite a convincing performance, wasn't it?" Seth said, taking a little bow. "And I just loved playing Phoebe."

"Wait a second. Aren't you supposed to be a *gas* or something?" I asked.

"PR story," he said. "This is Tinseltown, dear boy. Image is everything. Don't believe anything you read or hear in LA. Wasn't I fabulous as Phoebe, though? *I* think I was. I needed to get close to you, Daniel. To see if you posed any danger. You don't, by the way.

"Now, where were we? Oh yes. Your imminent death. *Imminent* means you're going to die *soon.*"

He slid his hand—which was more of a seashell-like talon—along my temple. All of a sudden, I felt seasick. Then came a black, despairing nausea. A centrifugal sucking sensation started deep at my core, as if a plug had been pulled at the bottom of my soul.

"My powers," I whimpered. "They're . . ."

"Being disconnected? Indeed," Seth said. "Good thing too. Your misguided thoughts matched with your kind of powers are a combination that is much too potentially dangerous to allow. Not to mention that you ruined my magnificent graveyard creation. That clinched it, I'm afraid. It was a masterwork, don't you agree? I was particularly fond of the odor of rotting flesh I was able to achieve. That's why I'm logging you off, son. Good-bye."

After another minute, the seashell claw withdrew. I lay motionless, hollowed out. I was surprised I could still breathe. I felt feverish, drugged, as Seth lifted me effortlessly in his arms.

"Night, Daniel," he said.

In Phoebe's voice, of course.

Chapter 48

AS IF FROM FAR AWAY, I heard the sound of traffic. *Traffic?*

As my head lolled back, I made out an upside-down Honda Odyssey with tinted black windows. It was the same minivan that I'd spotted in downtown la, carting around the drug-dealing children.

It's all coming together horribly, I thought as the van's door slid open. Then I was flying through the air before slamming painfully into the far wall.

Bang-up job, Dannyboy, I thought as my wrists and ankles were duct-taped. *Way to go get 'em. You are your father's son! You're definitely ready to battle Number 6 to the death. Yours!*

More ugly horse-heads—half a dozen—wearing muscle shirts and tracksuits and gold chains stared down at me with yellowish, cue-ball eyes.

"Meow," one of them said.

The rest burst into howling laughter. Hey, these were the same losers who'd trashed my house, the ones who'd done the cat attack.

"That's incredibly funny," I said as the van's tires squealed. "I know a good one too. This horse walks into a bar. Bartender says, 'Hey, buddy. Why the long face?' "

I was barely able to cover my head as a dozen shell talons clawed at my eyes.

"Slime 'im! Slime 'im! Slime 'im!" came an eerie chant. Whatever it meant, I didn't want it.

A particularly ugly, freak-show horse-face appeared a foot above mine. Something was oozing from the inside corners of its mouth hole.

I slammed my eyes shut as something warm and thick dripped onto my forehead and began to pool. The contents of my stomach rioted as I caught the spoiled clam-chowderish whiff of it.

I almost managed to close my mouth before the rancid, vomitizing ooze dripped off my nose, and onto my lips, and right down my throat.

By the way, don't say I didn't warn you back around page three that the story might get a little rough at times.

Chapter 49

I DON'T KNOW about you, but whenever I'm slimed and hog-tied in the stow-and-go seat well of a minivan, I tend to do a little soul-searching.

First of all, I was pretty angry with myself. I'd let Seth play me like an iPod Shuffle. I'd been *sooo* sure about how ninjalike and under the radar I was being, but now I realized Seth must have felt me the moment I set foot in la. He was Number 6, after all!

What else? Oh, yeah. I was in paralyzing fear of losing my life. Lots of kidnap victims can say they don't know what their captors will do to them, but I really, really didn't know. I mean, were these pus-headed aliens going to slime me again, or was it something worse? I figured . . . *worse*.

Then they started playing their music, which was a sophisticated form of torture in itself. The List of Alien Outlaws never said these freaks were fanatics of early eighties bands. We're talking Journey, Air Supply, Styx. And some group I'd never heard before called Yes that should have been called No. In my humble opinion, anyway.

The eardrum-walloping volume wouldn't have been so bad if these intergalactic thugs didn't have to sing along, like this was a karaoke van, banging their mallet-shaped heads back and forth and playing air guitar, air drums, air cymbals.

I just lay there in shock, gazing out the back window at the tops of telephone poles zipping by on our road trip to who-knew-where and who-knew-what.

I should have listened to my mother and father.

I should have listened to Dana.

I should have listened to Ergent Seth.

I'd been warned, hadn't I?

Chapter 50

IT WAS PITCH-BLACK when the silver van pulled off the highway to hell. I was barely able to catch the top of a DEATH VALLEY NATIONAL PARK sign that flashed in the brake lights out the back window.

I was yanked up roughly as we came to a stop about a half hour later. Outside in the headlights stood half a dozen weathered wood factory buildings.

Welcome to the middle of the middle of nowhere, I thought. So why did this scene seem extremely familiar to me?

"Hey, isn't this where they shot *Texas Chainsaw*

Massacre? The remake of the remake?" I said, thinking out loud.

"Very observant, Daniel," Seth said proudly. "A true masterpiece of the chain saw-wielding cannibal genre. At least you have good taste in bad movies. I told you, I was in the industry, didn't I? That remake was one of my finest awful films. Here, let me give you a tour of the shoot," he said. "No cameras, please!"

He ripped the duct tape off my feet, then dragged me out of the van by my hair. A very painful way to go.

I was pulled past a huge, rust-pocked metal tank into one of the buildings. Dozens of kids were inside, some of them in large cells and some chained to the walls.

I winced as I took in the faces. These were the same missing kids I'd seen from the file "Phoebe" had shown me in LA.

"So that part of the story was true," I said. "You really are off-loading kids from the earth. You're nothing but a slave trader."

"C'mon, that's not *all* I am," Seth said as he opened a cell door and kicked me inside. "Don't forget all the stealing, murdering, and drug dealing I do. Not to mention the hit movies I've made about zombies, cannibals, vampires, and cutting instruments."

I watched as Seth transformed himself into Phoebe Cook.

"Oh Danny. I need your help soooo much," he/she taunted. The rest of Seth's horse-head buddies slapped their thighs and broke up laughing.

Seth turned back into his vile and demonic self.

"Absurd logic on your part. Why would a girl as hot as Phoebe Cook need the help of a weak, stupid, substandard, inferior, about-to-be-extinct failure like you? Phoebe was a *test,* Daniel. You failed. Miserably. *Look* at you."

Whatever Seth had done to sap my power, it had worked. I was having trouble staying on my feet, or even focusing on his hideous horse's head.

"Now that we've come face-to-face, Seth," I said, staring steadily into his reddish-brown eyes, "my only regret is that you're not the insectlike lowlife who actually killed my folks."

"Oh, I just might be their killer after all," he roared.

"No, you're not," I said with a shake of my head. "I marked that miscreant on his skull after he murdered my mom and dad. The creature who took out my parents, the one who is going to pay with his life, is The Prayer. You're only *sixth* on my List, Seth. Dream on!"

"Isn't that interesting?" Seth said. "You learn something new and useful every day. Speaking of which, maybe I can tell you something that you didn't know, Mr. Smartass. *You're* Number 1 on the Hit Parade of every alien currently residing on this backworld of a planet. We were hunting for *you*, young Daniel X. And I just won the jackpot. That's why you're still alive. I want to show off my prize. I won, you lost. Maybe I'll drag you from galaxy to galaxy—*in captivity*."

Chapter 51

"YOU'VE BEEN A WOEFUL, pitiful dupe all along," said Seth. "I guess it's to be expected, given what dullards your parents were. What were their names—Graff and Atrelda? Who can even remember? Who cares? The way I hear it, those two were actually too stupid to let live. They practically murdered themselves."

If I'd been in fighting shape, I would have ripped a hole through the steel mesh to get at Seth's lopsided face. My parents had been selfless protectors and friends of humanity, horrifically murdered by a misshapen monster without a conscience.

"I'll admit it. You got me," I said. "For the most part, you really did keep your thoughts consistent with a normal girl like Phoebe Cook. It was a pretty brilliant operation."

"Please. Pulling the wool over your eyes was as easy as beating you at chess," Seth said. "But what's with the 'for the most part' rubbish?"

I looked at him as if I were suddenly bored . . . which I definitely was not.

"At Phoebe's house that night, remember our sleepover? You let down your guard. You blew it, Seth. *You had a dream.* I scanned it. At first I thought it was a really odd nightmare coming from Phoebe, but now I realize that it was *your* dream. It all makes perfect sense. I know what your greatest fears are, Seth. Your deepest vulnerabilities, even what you're going to do next. You'll never get away with it. Won't happen."

Seth stared at me even more dead-faced than usual, seemingly confused for the moment.

His cronies were staring at him now, waiting for their leader to strike back.

"What dream?" Seth said. "What was in my dream?"

"That's for me to know and you to agonize about, you donkey-faced freak," I said. "I'll give you a hint. *Dumb-Dumb,*" I whispered.

It sounded like a couple of grenades going off in the

cage as Seth kicked it again and again. I stifled laughter, then decided the heck with it, and let myself crack up.

"*Dumb-Dumb*," I repeated.

Chapter 52

"YOU READ MY DREAM, did you? I'm truly impressed."

Suddenly Seth had a smile on his face. An awful, pinched smile, matched with an even more heartless gleam in his dark, demonic eyes.

"Wait! Maybe *you'll* be impressed with something I have in the back room," he said, clapping a claw to his head as if he'd been forgetting something. "Hold on, I'll be right back. Don't you dare go anywhere. You'll love this."

I didn't like the sound of that one bit. Even his disgusting followers looked worried when he shouldered his way past them and disappeared down a long, dingy hallway.

They actually dove out of the way when he returned a moment later. He was holding something above his head. My eyes locked on it. Oh boy! An Opus 24/24 assault rifle.

"Say hello to my little friend," Seth said. "Nothing like the cool steel of an Opus 24/24. And what a coincidence. I could be wrong, but isn't this the same sort of weapon that did in your dear departed mother and father? I believe it is."

The door of my cage screeched like a banshee as Seth flung it open. A chill raced down the ridge of my spine. Everyone was deathly quiet—the kids, Seth's thugs, even Seth.

Slowly he raised the deadly rifle to his shoulder.

"What are you going to do now? Shoot me?" I asked with a fake smile.

A bloom of fire burst from the gun's barrel. What felt like dynamite exploded inside my stomach.

"Good guess," Seth said with a smile as I flew backward about fifteen feet and landed spread-eagled on the floor.

What can I tell you about getting gut-shot? It's bad. About as bad as it gets. Excruciating is the tip of the iceberg. I could actually feel the bullet deep in my stomach, feel its heat, feel it burning into the torn tissue that surrounded it.

I slapped my hand to the wound as blood—red blood, not green or anything—started pouring out from between my ring finger and pinkie.

The most sickening sadness laced the pain as my vision started to blur, then flicker. I wondered if this was how my mother and father felt just before they died.

Talk about having a sucky last day, I thought, as I fell away into darkness.

And I had kind of liked Terra Firma too.

I would miss night baseball, sno-cones, Spider-Man, the Winter Olympics . . .

White Castle sliders, Bart Simpson, did I mention sno-cones? . . .

Chapter 53

I DON'T KNOW how long it was before I came to—I wasn't even sure if coming to was what I was doing. All I knew for sure was that there was a worried face floating maybe a foot above me. The innocent face of a seven- or eight-year-old girl.

I would have believed she was an angel—except for the terrible waves of pain throbbing in my stomach.

I looked down and saw that the girl had balled up my shirt and stuffed it into my wound. A tear rolled out of my eye onto the stone floor. Abducted, terrified, and most likely in shock, this little girl had probably saved my life.

Gestures like that were why humans were worth saving, I thought. Or even worth dying for.

"Thank you," I whispered. "These ugly horse-heads better watch their step. They're starting to get on my nerves."

"Mine too," said the girl.

"*Hey, you!* What do you think you're doing in there?" came a voice. One of the aliens was crouching by the cell door. "Didn't I tell everyone not to touch him?"

The little girl stared at him like a deer frozen in headlights, at least the way I've always imagined that cliché looks.

"Hey, give me back my wallet," I croaked at her, loud enough for the thug to hear.

"Oh, why didn't you say you were just robbing him?" the guard said, turning away. "In that case, go for it. You humans are lower than dirt. Tear each other apart. Go for it."

Chapter 54

I SPENT the better part of the next hour lying there on the cold stone floor, writhing in pain, probably close to death. I'd lost what seemed like quarts of blood, and my intestines and vital organs must have been ripped apart by the gun blast.

Gut-shot down in the salt mine, I thought, starting to shake a little with the agony. Gee, my life had become the title of a country-and-western song.

A short time later, a door banged open and a couple of guards charged in. They were carrying electric stun guns.

"For me? You shouldn't have."

"Get moving, you filthy mammals," one of the aliens yelled as he herded together the Earth kids I was sharing the chamber with. The little girl who'd helped me started to sob.

"Hey, guys, look! This one's sprung a leak." The alien laughed as he waved the cattle prod next to her tear-filled face. "I can't believe we actually get paid to have this much fun."

"You too, *worm*," Seth said, tapping a couple of thousand volts near my face. "Get up! Get moving. Hold your intestines in."

I probably should have been in an icu, but I shot to my feet and stumbled out of the cage. No way I'd let them know how badly I was hurt.

"Nice acting job!" Seth said, and roared with laughter. "You could have been in one of my films. As an extra."

It was pitch-black outside in the desert. And freezing cold. At two, maybe three o'clock in the morning.

Why did I have the feeling that we weren't going on a nature walk?

Chapter 55

AS I TURNED to my right, I saw that the desert sky was filled with stars in every direction. Except one. Above the eastern mountains, there was a . . . hole in the sky. A hole that was moving closer and getting larger and larger by the second.

The hairs on the back of my neck stood at full, parade-ground attention.

The object hovering about fifty feet above me was black as the night itself, and about the size of a football stadium. I don't know who started that UFO saucer nonsense, but they must have been nearsighted. This ship was undoubtedly rectangular, like a Dumpster. Or a giant coffin.

It just hung there above us, ominously floating. There was a disturbance in the air as some kind of energy field pulsated loudly across its massive length.

Then a telescopic column, possibly an elevator, dropped from its belly into the ground.

Some of the kids started crying, and I called out, "Don't worry, it's nothing. It's probably just E.T."

The elevator thingy landed less than thirty feet from where I stood. A hydraulic hum followed. Then a doorway opened.

Inside, a particularly huge and ugly horse-head in a black uniform was smiling, showing cobralike teeth.

"Hey there, kiddies. Want to go for a ride, huh-huh-huh?" he said in a pretty good imitation of SpongeBob SquarePants.

All of us abductees stared at the alien in the doorway. Then we stared at each other. And then, as if we'd finally reached a silent consensus, we started to scream at the top of our lungs.

Chapter 56

THE RIDE UP in the crowded alien elevator made all of
the smaller kids scream again. It was like an *upward* free
fall, or bungee jumping in reverse. I can tell you this—the
open wound that was my stomach really appreciated the
ride.

The back of the elevator opened, and we were hauled
out into the mother ship.

Somehow the hot, cramped inside managed to be more
horrible and despair-inducing than the grim exterior had
promised. Those *Star Trek* writers were bugging when
they dreamed up the dentist's office-like *Enterprise,* I

thought, as I looked around. Water and steam dripped from tangles of overhead ducts. The floors were slick with what appeared to be oil and discarded garbage. The place looked like a boiler room and a landfill combined.

A blast of hot air from somewhere swept across my face, and I caught the stink. Think the world's hugest bus station bathroom.

We were pushed through a metal detector-like apparatus. Seth came over to me as it beeped. He ripped my List computer out of my backpack.

"You won't be needing this," he said, tucking it under his arm, "ever, *ever* again."

We were sprayed with some type of stinging gas, stuffed into gray jumpsuits, and shackled together with leg chains. Very neighborly.

I turned toward one of the portholes when I heard a low rumble coming from somewhere inside the ship. Down below, the desert mountains were getting smaller and smaller at a mind-blowing speed. What was crazy was that, unlike in the elevator, there wasn't the slightest sense of motion.

About three seconds later, there was Terra Firma, my beloved planet Earth. Even under the circumstances, its grandeur took my breath away.

The astronauts had never communicated how completely lonely it looks, though. Sad, blue, and sort of helpless against the endless void of space. I watched it get smaller and smaller, and then—with what felt like a pinch in my heart—Earth was gone.

Chapter 57

A COUPLE MORE black uniforms smacked and kicked us down a corridor toward a scary grinding sound that made me think of a transformer eating scrap metal. The hall opened into a tremendous chamber, and I had to wipe my eyes to make sure I wasn't imagining things.

Down here were tiers upon tiers of cages and machines. At the machines, humans—mostly kids—were hard at work. They were hand rolling cigarettes, putting what looked like torture devices together, sewing animal skins into coats.

There were a few older humans too. *The floor managers*

of hell, I thought. One of them was shaking a tiny Chinese kid back and forth against an industrial sewing machine. The kid was so dead-eyed, he wasn't even crying.

The ship was some kind of flying child slavery sweatshop, I understood. A prison, a slave ship, and a sweatshop all rolled into one.

It really was hell, I thought. We'd actually arrived.

"Home sweet home," one of the aliens said as he doled out the manacled kids to floor managers waiting by escalators. "No iPods or PlayStation 3's here, you spoiled, hairless monkeys. Prepare to learn the true meaning of the expression 'working your fingers to the bone.' You've heard of tough love? *Welcome to tough hate.*"

"We have different accommodations for you, Daniel," Seth said in my ear as he personally dragged me over another catwalk and down a filthy gray corridor. "You actually get your own room. Just in case you're more *dangerous* than you seem to be."

A door zipped open in a wall, and I flew through the air into a pitch-black cell. "Anything you need, *scream.*"

Chapter 58

FOR A WHILE, I did my best to stay upbeat. *The night is darkest before the dawn*, I reminded myself. *Every cloud has a silver lining. What doesn't kill you makes you stronger. I will live to fight another day.*

Yeah, right, I thought as the bullet in my abdomen continued to send out unrelenting pulses of agony.

Makes you stronger; cripples you forever. Flip a coin.

I couldn't believe how overly confident I'd been. I'd actually thought I could defeat Ergent Seth. But I was a loser, complete and utter. I guess it was a family tradition.

"You are not a loser!" said a voice. "Not always, anyway."

It must have been my fever. I was hearing voices now. Was it Glenda, the good witch? Or maybe Pinocchio's friend the Blue Fairy?

"I've been brave, truthful, and unselfish," I slurred. "Now make me a real boy."

I guess several hours held captive by Seth was my mental limit. *E.T. ready for funny farm.*

I opened my eyes and saw that it was Dana. Well, sort of.

She was coming in hazily, kind of two-dimensional. I could actually see *through* her. How weird was that? She seemed like a ghost. Or an angel. Maybe I was dead and had gone to heaven?

"You are not a loser, Daniel," Dana insisted again, her matchless blue eyes on the verge of tears. Then a second later, she was past the verge.

"Oh, Daniel," she sobbed. "You can't die."

"Don't," I said. "You can't cry, Dana. My heart can stand pretty much anything except seeing you cry."

"But *look* at you. I've never seen you like this. What happened to you? Besides that . . . Phoebe Cook flirtation. What was *that* about? *God,* Daniel."

The last thing I was going to do was tell her that I was gut-shot.

171

"Seth," I said. That about summed it up.

"What about your powers? Don't tell me they're gone. Please don't tell me that."

"Dana, c'mon," I said. "Of course I still have my powers."

"Maybe you'd feel better if you got up off that cold floor and moved around," Dana said, offering me her hand.

Maybe she was right. Maybe all this agony was in my head. With super effort, I climbed up on my knees. Then I dropped facedown, cracked my head on the hard cell floor, and passed out cold.

Chapter 59

WHEN I WOKE AGAIN, I don't know how much later, I noticed that I wasn't bleeding anymore. I wasn't up for a footrace with a pickup truck or anything, but I felt like maybe in another hour or so, I could do something incredible. Like, say, sit up.

I was about to give it a shot when the cell door clanged open, and Seth waltzed in. In his claw was an iron bowl of some slop that smelled like rotting fish and looked like macaroni and eye cheese.

"Here, boy," he said, clucking his tongue as he dropped the bowl next to my head. "Oh, what's wrong?

Does the little doggie have a tum-tum ache? Don't want to play epic hero anymore? No more a-hunting-aliens-we-will-go? I came down here just to watch your suffering and humiliation. The thing about moments of triumph, you want to make them last!"

"Please don't hurt me," I said, shivering. "Please."

"Oh, don't worry," Seth said as he squatted down to get a better look at my misery. "I will."

That's precisely when I manifested Willy, Joe, Dana, and Emma into the open doorway behind the big horse-headed creep.

That's right. *Never give up, never say die, live in complete denial.* I even remembered to dress them in the filthy gray jumpsuits that were all the rage with the abducted tween-age slave set this season.

I told you I was feeling a little, teensy bit better. It's hard to keep a good Alien Hunter down. I think it was the sleep that had done it. I'd recharged enough to work at least a little of my power. Maybe five percent.

I watched my gang hoof it out of my cell and down the corridor of the ship.

"You are pathetic, do you know that?" Seth continued. "You actually thought you could come after me? And win? I even warned you. But losers such as yourself never learn, I suppose. Losers like you are never satisfied until someone actually hands them their head."

"I should have listened to you," I moaned, crying. Shia LaBeouf couldn't have done a better acting job, not even with Steven Spielberg directing. "Please, please," I said, writhing for effect. "I'll do anything you want."

Seth merely smiled. "Of course you will."

Chapter 60

FOR THE NEXT couple of hours, I lay flat on my back in my cell with my eyes closed. What with all I'd been through, I was putting up my feet and taking a major breather.

Yeah, right! Actually, I was busy communicating telepathically with my friends as they searched the ship for a way out, or at least a way to strike back at Seth and his goons.

First off I watched as Willy searched level upon level for any sign of a lifeboat or an escape pod, but unfortunately there was nothing. It was a Hail Mary, I knew, because even if he found one, there was no way of knowing how to operate it or even which was the direction back to Earth. Willy tried to get near what he thought might be the bridge, but it was crawling with heavily armed mutant horse-faces.

On the main slave factory floor, Joe and Emma discovered that there were chains and pallets underneath all the worktables. The kid slaves worked and slept in the same five square feet.

But Joe and Emma did manage to do something positive. They sat with about twenty or so abducted girls gathered around them. Emma had snagged some yarn from one of the sweatshop shelves, and she was showing them how to make friendship bracelets. Leave it to Emma to find a silver lining just about anywhere.

The most heart-shredding of the psychic podcasts came from Dana. She had spoken to one of the prisoners, a pale Asian American boy who had more than a passing resemblance to the ghost kid from *The Grudge*.

"How long have you been here?" Dana asked. "Can you tell me that?"

The kid looked right through her.

"Dunno."

"Months? Years?"

"Dunno."

"Where are the older kids?" Dana said.

A look of horror invaded the kid's face.

"Taken away," he whispered. He began sobbing as Dana picked him up and put him in her lap. "Sold."

Of course, I thought. As if breaking their spirits wasn't enough, Seth had put the kids on the auction block and sold them to whoever—or *whatever*—could come up with the highest price.

Maybe that was why I was being kept alive—to be sold at auction. *How much for an Alien Hunter, slightly used? With five percent of his former powers?*

"You're going to be okay," Dana said, hugging the boy as tears rolled down her cheeks. "We're going to get you out of here and back home. Hey, you want to play I spy? I'll go first. I spy with my little eye something cute. *You.*"

The kid actually giggled. How do you like that? Leave it to her. Even in hell, Dana could make people laugh.

Okay, then, what had I learned? Fact one: there was no resistance against the impossibly cruel alien creeps. Fact two: there was no possibility for escape.

I reminded myself for the millionth time to never underestimate an opponent again. Oh, wait. What was I thinking? There wasn't going to be an again.

Chapter 61

I WAS EATING an imaginary cherry sno-cone—which helped my spirits more than you might think. I was planning on an imaginary lemon-and-lime one next.

"Bet's to you, Daniel," Pork Chop said, peering at me over her massive pile of chips. "Quit stalling and lose the hand already."

If you think regular solitary confinement is boring, you should try it on an alien spaceship. That's why I decided to host a family World Series of Poker tournament in my cell.

I guess I was feeling a little better. In the special power

sense, at least. I was able to manifest my parents and sister, the poker table, cards, some chips, sno-cones.

"And on our left, the Danster continues to hold up the game," my sister complained. "And to slurp in the most disgusting way imaginable."

"I call," I said, turning over my aces.

All six of them.

"What the—?" Pork Chop said in outrage. She picked up two of my aces and shook them in my face. "This is outrageous. I don't care if you are delirious."

"That's the ace of crosses and the ace of cats," I said proudly.

"Those cards don't exist," Pork Chop said. "Those *suits* don't even exist."

"Daniel, c'mon. That's not like you," my mom said.

"Gee, Mom," I said, clutching my aching stomach. "I guess I haven't been in the best of moods since Seth gave me this new belly button here."

An overwhelming sense of sadness and anger had finally enveloped me. Here I was about to be executed or maybe something worse—and what was I doing? Sitting here and taking it.

"Who am I kidding with this garbage?" I yelled. "Pork Chop, listen to me! You think cheating at cards is a shocker? I know something that'll blow your mind. . . . *You're not real!* I invent you, create you, bring you into being. I daydream you like the alien that I am. Mom and Dad aren't real either!"

"What are you? Crazy?" Brenda said, making a face. "Who died and made you God? Explain that one to me."

A chilling realization came to me then. *I knew who Brenda really was.* And why I could manifest her so easily.

"Okay, here's your explanation. Ready? You used to be real, but you were killed."

My sister's face was drained of its color.

"What do you mean? I feel perfectly fine. When did this happen?"

"When I was three a killer came to our house. His name is The Prayer. Mom must have been pregnant with you. When she died, you died."

Pork Chop turned to my mom and dad. Tears beaded in her eyes. "He's lying," she said. "I don't want to be dead. I don't want you both to be dead."

I looked across the room, where my mother and father were hugging Pork Chop. Both of them were crying too.

And then they were gone.

Chapter 62

I WAS SLUMPED over in my cell, feeling awful about what I'd said to Pork Chop, when I sensed wraithlike movement on the other side of my cell door. Then Seth entered with a contingent of formal-looking, uniformed alien guards. Now I felt even worse. If I was murdered, I'd never be able to tell Pork Chop how sorry I was.

I was herded into a large, high-ceilinged chamber crowded with a couple dozen horse-heads in black smocks, working at computer consoles.

Was this the execution chamber?

My mind reeled, coming up with a couple dozen

horrendous ways in which I would now be put to death. I gritted my teeth and erased all the bad images. I wasn't going to give Seth the satisfaction of seeing me afraid.

"Get it over with, Seth," I said. "Do your worst. I can take it."

"You think so? Put his home up on the big screen," Seth commanded.

I turned as a soccer field-sized wall seemed to vaporize and a star-sprawled view of space appeared.

Oh, I thought. This wasn't the execution chamber. It was the bridge of the spaceship. Whoops, I'd jumped to the wrong conclusion. I liked this one a whole lot better.

The view on the screen seemed to pan to the left. I gasped! Filling the screen was Earth in all its massive, beautiful glory.

"Why have we come back?" I asked. "And why is Terra Firma greenish at the edges? What have you done now, Seth?"

"Come back? Did you hear this fool?" Seth called out to the other aliens. "Of course, we just went for a seventeen-light-year spin around the block. That's not Earth, idiot. I said *you* were home. Welcome to Alpar Nok, your home world, jackass."

Alpar Nok? I thought, staring at the green-tinged planet. *My home?*

The screen tilted suddenly, and the shining green

planet on it got larger and larger as we approached in a hurry.

My poker face crumbled as we blasted through clouds and an ocean appeared. An ocean, calm and limitless and filled with the purest, bluest water I'd ever seen.

I felt it then, a kind of warming of my soul. I could hardly breathe. I couldn't take my eyes away from this miracle.

I was home.

Chapter 63

I WAS STILL DUMBFOUNDED as Seth and his security contingent of armed mutant killers escorted me through the bowels of the ship and toward the landing elevator.

A million questions and feelings rushed through me at once. *What would my people look like? Would anyone know me? Did they all have powers like mine? Did I have actual family still living here?*

"You may wonder why I brought you home," Seth prattled on with his fancy English accent. "I'm such a show-off. Love to rub it in. I wanted your race to see that their defeat was complete across the universe. All hail the

185

returning conquered *loser!* That's *you*, by the way."

Unfortunately Seth was right. My hands were shackled behind me, then I was shoved roughly into the elevator car.

We plummeted, and almost instantly slammed to a sudden stop. The forward ramp automatically dropped down, kicking up dust. I squinted through it as I was pushed out and . . .

Felt panic. Huge *Perfect Storm* waves of horror and dread and shock.

No! I thought. *This can't be my home.*

For mile upon mile, as far as my eye could see, corkscrewed metal girders and wrecked vehicles poked out from mountainous piles of scorched rubble. The few buildings that were still standing were warped, shattered, windowless. The prevailing sound was the whistle of wind over tumbled bricks. From horizon to horizon lay the demolished remains of a massive city, one that had been as big as New York or London.

Staring at the destruction, I stood frozen with despair. Grief for my people and my ruined world filled me. Seth had gotten me yet again, I realized. *Hey, look, Daniel. Here's your home planet. Oh, I forgot to mention, it's been leveled.*

Chapter 64

I CAUGHT HIM staring at me, a mirthful smile on his fetid alien face. *He's fooled me twice,* I thought with a shake of my head. *Shame on me.*

Twenty feet below the rim of the elevated landing ramp was what looked like a derailed bullet train. Someone had scrawled DEATH TO ERGENT SETH in its dust-covered side.

"*You* did this," I said, turning to Seth. It wasn't a question.

Seth took a long cigar out of his pocket and lit it with a gold Zippo as he winked at me.

"I know," he said, blinking as he shook his head at the desolate vista. "Unreal, isn't it? Sometime, even *I* can't believe it. I mean, ever since I was little, I always dreamed of committing mass destruction. But on this kind of scale? It's more than even I had a right to expect."

Seth raised a claw and saluted his handiwork. Half a mile away, a massive pit was being carved out of the rubble. Insectlike machines of the same green-gray metal as the spacecraft were moving around and around in slow circles. There were more pits in the distance beyond it, and more busy insectile machines.

"They're called World Harvesters, my race's greatest invention," Seth said proudly.

"They'll chew through anything—rock, garbage, dead bodies, you name it—and remove every atom of valuable minerals and elements. It took half a million years for your people to build the city of Bryn Spi, the shining jewel of your planet. It took me one and a half hours to blow it into a billion shiny pieces. And by this time next year— and this is my favorite part—it will look like nothing ever stood here at all."

My heart seemed to be unfastening inside my chest. "Where is everyone?" I asked.

"Your fellow Alparians? The few who are still alive scurry through the ruins like rats. They have no powers, no hope, no reason to live, really. But still they stumble on. Pathetic."

Seth shook his head in disgust.

"Protectors of the Universe?" he said, tapping the ash from his cigar with one of his talons. "Guess they should have worried more about protecting themselves."

Chapter 65

"WHAT DO YOU MEAN, Protectors of the Universe?" I asked.

"You *are* clueless, aren't you?" Seth said. "I keep forgetting you had all this thrust on you at three years of age. Behold, Alpar Nok, the home of the Alien Hunters, the universe's answer to injustice and evil! Your parents were sent to Earth to protect the oh-so-special humans from the Outer Ones, as they like to call us.

"Because a few pathetic Alparians were born with some ability to manipulate the universal force, it was thought you could protect the good from the evil. As if good and evil aren't just fairy tales made up for small children. There are the *strong* and then there are the *weak*."

I looked out at the ruined city again. Seth and his buddies had left just enough standing for me to see how amazing it must have been.

Fragments of exotic spires, pyramids, domes, pagodas, minarets, columns, and obelisks peeked out in every direction. Right next to us was a giant sculpted building that looked like a hundred-story violin made of glass and metal. Now it leaned precariously because a huge hole had been blown in its base.

Wait a second, I thought. It was leaning toward us.

Maybe that was a good thing.

Chapter 66

IT COULD HAVE BEEN the air of my homeland, or maybe a coincidence, but ever since I'd stepped foot on Alpar Nok, power had been flowing into me. I could feel my energy surging as if I'd just downed about a dozen Red Bulls. Can you imagine it?

There was no time to think this over. I had to do something outrageous and unexpected before Seth found out that my abilities were coming back. *This* qualified as pretty outrageous, I figured. The question bouncing around my head was whether outrageous equaled really dumb or really ingenious.

I scanned the already weakened base of the building that was tilted toward us. I did some quick calculations in my head. Checked the math. Then I unleashed everything I had at the thinnest part of one of the bent girders.

Here goes nothing. Or, I guess, everything!

The landing party of horse-skulls turned as the girder sheared with the loudest imaginable *crack*.

There was a deafening groan as the tower shuddered, then—*TIMBER!*—it collapsed against the side of the ship's landing shaft. Actually, it disintegrated the shaft.

Seth's cigar went flying. Next I shattered my shackles with a violent flex of my shoulders. And because I couldn't resist, I threw a roundhouse punch into Seth's snout. He. Didn't. Even. Flinch.

Then I leaped off the ramp, hitting the rubble at a run. Or should I say, *dead* run?

I turned into the nearest alley, then skidded to an immediate, lifesaving stop.

I was right at the edge of one of the strip-mining pits, a chasm at least three or four hundred feet straight down, maybe a city block wide. I had missed falling into the pit by inches!

My chest was heaving as I spotted what appeared to be a tunnel opening on the opposite wall of the chasm, twenty or thirty yards across. I backed up and yelled—for extra strength, and to distract me from my fears. And common sense, maybe? Then I ran forward and jumped off the edge, using every ounce of energy I had.

I made it by inches—and then I heard Opus 24/24 gunfire from above.

Bullets rained down everywhere, burrowing into the ground like steel fists.

I turbo-crawled maybe twenty feet into the darkness and waited an eternity—until the thunderous gunfire finally stopped.

Then I heard the cackle of Seth's laughter. It echoed against the walls of my planet's version of Death Valley.

"Go ahead, run-*un-un*," Seth yelled, echoes trampling all over his slimy words. "You're a cockroach in a dump-*ump-ump*. Fall on your face! Stay here in this graveyard if you like-*ike-ike*. Does it matter? You're just one more useless slave-*ave-ave!* Welcome home, loser-*ser-ser!*"

I took the time to yell back, "Kiss my butt-*utt-utt*."

Then I ran until, finally, I was a blur.

Chapter 67

I DON'T KNOW how long it was that I ran, then jogged, then stumbled through the totally unfamiliar semi-darkness. Unfortunately my stomach wound was bleeding again.

I found some kind of monorail track thing and followed it for at least a couple of hours. You wouldn't think that a city could be so big, but Bryn Spi seemed to go on forever.

I think I actually fell asleep walking at one point.

The next thing I knew, I was waking up as I heard

somebody, or some *thing*, breathing in the darkness above me.

"Hey!" a kid's voice came as I reached up and grabbed a head of longish hair.

A flashlight came on next.

"Lay off! Let me go!" a dirty-faced kid yelled, waving his flashlight. He was emaciated, dressed in filthy rags, and furious with me.

"And what do you think you're doing, hovering over me like that?" I asked him.

"I practically tripped over you lying like a rotty corpse in the middle of the tunnel, you idiot. Leggo my hair now!"

I released my grip.

"Smart move, sucker," the kid said, frowning and rubbing his scalp. "Nobody messes with Bem. Even the Outer Ones better watch their step with me."

"Oh, I'm sure they do, Bem. They would never mess with the likes of you."

I stood for a moment just gazing at the boy. I couldn't believe I'd finally come into contact with one of my people!

"Quit staring," he said. "You're creeping me out."

Okay, then, I thought. *I guess all of us aren't telepathic.*

"Is your mom or dad around?" I asked the boy.

"Died on FirstStrike. It's just me and Kulay now. Kulay's my sister."

"Where do you live?"

"In Undertown, of course. Where else? Where *you* been?"

"Will you show me?"

The feisty kid squinted at me and put up his fists. "Why should I?"

I concentrated and levitated Bem a foot or so off the ground.

"Okay, that's a good reason," he said, and started to walk. *"Keep up!"*

The tunnel we traveled through gradually began to widen. More tunnels branched to the right and left until finally we stepped into a massive chamber. One, I noticed, that was crowded with people.

My people.

Maybe I could find someone who knew my parents! I thought as I approached the crowd. Imagine if I had a family? Real aunts and uncles and cousins?

It didn't take long for my hope to wither. Undertown wasn't doing so hot. Every inch of the chamber was covered with crude wooden and cardboard shanties.

"Numbdown, git sum, git sum!" called a tough-looking kid around Bem's age. He was waving dirty vials in my face as I passed. Numbdown must have been Alpar Nok's answer to crack.

I smacked the drugs away from my face onto the concrete floor and crushed them under my sneaker.

"Common sense!" I said to the kid: "Git sum, git sum."

Chapter 68

BEM AND KULAY'S HOME was a cavelike structure about the size of a toolshed, with a rusty drainpipe in the corner for a toilet. And, I think, a *sink*.

Kulay turned out to be four and was doing about as well as her "big" brother. She was pretty, but thin and bony, and one of her feet looked like it had been crushed recently and had healed wrong.

"Take me," Kulay said to her brother as he opened the corrugated sheet of metal they used as a door. "Take me. Take me. Take me."

She didn't seem to notice that I was there, and I was

curious about where it was that she wanted to go.

"I'm busy, Kulay," Bem said, exasperated. "Can't you see that? Can't you see *him?*"

I searched the pockets of my jumpsuit and came out with a crushed blueberry energy bar I'd managed to keep hidden from the horse-heads. I tore it open and gave them each half.

That seemed to win Bem over. I actually saw him drop his permanent scowl for a second as he chewed.

"Where does Kulay want to go?" I asked.

"It's . . . the only good thing left in this crummy city, I guess. It's . . . hard to describe. You have to see it. Do you want to? Anyway, she won't stop bugging me until we go."

"Take me, take me!" I said in response, and even Kulay grinned this time. Cute kid. I wondered if she was one of my cousins.

Chapter 69

I LIFTED KULAY, who weighed next to nothing, and followed Bem out the hole in a wall that served as a door. We walked to the outskirts of the ramshackle underground town and went through a busted gate into a narrow corridor.

We walked for maybe an hour through a labyrinth of corridors until we came to a set of metal stairs.

After climbing seven stories, Bem opened a door into a huge concrete room filled with silent, turbinelike machines.

Behind one of them was a circular door in a wide pipe with a spin valve opener.

"What are you doing?" I said as Bem went down on all fours, spun the valve, then pulled open the door.

"You'll see," Kulay said with a giggle as she crawled out of my arms and into the pipe. *"Take me, take me!"* she shouted.

Bem was right on her tail.

I shook my head, but I followed along.

Trap? I wondered.

I had trusted people before and look where it had gotten me. Phoebe Cook had turned out to be Ergent Seth. So who were these two kids?

I crawled right behind Bem, close enough to grab him if I had to. Well, I wriggled, if you want to get technical, since my shoulders just barely fit.

Suddenly I heard Kulay yell, *"Wheeee!"* and then there was a loud, wet splash.

"What the –?" But it was too late. The pipe tilted downward, and I was sliding, then free-falling.

I didn't have time to scream before I belly-flopped into a humongous, double-Olympic-sized indoor swimming pool.

I came to the surface, gasping.

This was totally amazing, like nothing I'd ever seen.

All around me, shafts of light streamed in through cathedral-sized windows of translucent glass.

The unchlorinated water was the cleanest I'd ever

drunk, let alone swum in. I suddenly felt like I could run a marathon.

I floated on my back as I looked up at the soaring dome of the ceiling. Intricately drawn on it was what looked like this world's largest Renaissance painting.

In the center of the mural, kids ran and played games involving complex and very colorful kites. The detail was extraordinary, like nothing I had ever seen on Earth, even at the Louvre and the Met.

I shook my head. I could have stayed there for weeks and weeks. If this kind of craftsmanship was evident in public pools, I wondered, what did they display in the museums?

Kulay spit a spray of water at me before hopping out the side like a little seal.

"Come on," she said, giggling. "Take me, take me!"

"What? Aren't we here?" I asked.

"*The pool?* You haven't seen anything yet," Bem said. "The pool was just to clean ourselves up a bit."

Chapter 70

I FOLLOWED the two of them, dripping wet, down a gallery walled with strange but beautiful glass windows. At its arched end, I suddenly stopped.

Look out, ground, I thought, *here comes my jaw!*

It took me a second to process what I was seeing. Think of Central Park. Okay? Now imagine the universe's biggest solarium built *around it.*

We're talking trees, softly rolling grass hills, cobblestone strolling paths, ponds, beneath a sky of bright, startling blue.

"Hey, wait a second, Bem. This doesn't make sense.

Why wasn't this destroyed like everything else?"

"The sky isn't real. It's a dome," Bem said.

"My dad told me it's made of a special glass that does something to light, lets it in but not out. Long ago, there was a war and the Children's Park was bombed, so they made this new one indoors. Even the Outer Ones couldn't find it. Even Ergent Seth couldn't!"

"We've met," I told Bem and left it at that.

What caught my eye next was a massive gray stone structure. I followed Bem and Kulay around a curving path and up its mystery steps. When I got to the top and saw what was beyond the front gates, I felt tears brim in my eyes.

All is not lost, said a voice in my head.

It was a zoo.

But not just any zoo. Inside the gates was a large viewing platform, and beyond it, on grassland fields to the left and right, were *elephants!*

Chapter 71

AFRICAN ONES! Indian ones! Calves! Mothers! Herd upon herd of elephants. There were hundreds, maybe thousands. *Definitely thousands.*

I thought I was going to need a defibrillator when I saw what was rolling in the mud to my immediate left.

Trunk, check.

Ginormous ears, check.

Woolly brown fur? Check!

Twenty feet away I had spotted a family of cute, short-trunked creatures.

They were mastodons! Had to be.

They were supposed to be *extinct,* but I guess that was just on Earth.

I stood there feeling electroshocked as a female approached. She was twice as big as the largest elephant I'd ever seen on Earth. Forty, maybe fifty thousand pounds.

Her head came above the ten-foot-high viewing platform. Her trunk was as thick as a telephone pole.

Then—she extended her trunk to me.

How do you do? she said in my mind. *My name is Chordata.*

For a second, I was unable to think straight, or breathe, actually.

I'd never communicated telepathically with an elephant before. I finally recovered a little and shook her trunk.

My name is . . . I started to say.

Daniel. Yes, I remember you from when you were a baby. You used to come here every day with your mother. We would communicate like this.

You're the only two-leg I ever met who was able to. An elephant never forgets, you know. And never ever forgets a friend. I was very sad when you left. But happy now that you have come back. How are you doing, Daniel?

I'm pretty much blown away right this second, Chordata, I thought, smiling as I stared into her beautiful violet eyes.

So this was why I loved elephants so much?

I see you've met those two little monkeys Bem and Kulay. Cute, aren't they?

I nodded, then lost my breath as Chordata's massive knee bowed—and she offered us her back.

Please, come with me and meet the others. You can trust me, Daniel. An elephant never betrays a friend.

Bem, Kulay, and I were all able to ride on her rolling ship of a back, with room to spare.

From all over the grassland, elephants started moving toward us. One of the mastodons trumpeted, and then from everywhere the others started joining in, a happy symphony of welcome.

Soon we were in a crush of them, shaking and high-fiving offered trunks. Feelings of euphoria almost knocked me into the tall blond grass as their life-affirming, warm presence soaked right through me.

"Wow! I never did this before!" Kulay shrieked ecstatically. She was vibrating up and down like a gum machine bouncy ball. "I'm the luckiest kid in the world! I'm the luckiest kid in the world!"

I ruffled her hair as more and more elephants paraded over, their trunks buzzing out note after brilliant note.

"No," I said. "You're the luckiest kid in *two* worlds. Here, and a place called Earth."

Chapter 72

I CAN DIE NOW, I thought, as we headed back into Undertown three hours later. The afternoon I'd just spent was worth getting gut-shot, I decided. Worth getting duped by Seth.

Not only was hanging with Chordata and the other elephants the coolest thing I'd ever done, it was pretty much the coolest thing anybody has ever done.

I would have gladly lived there like a wild elephant boy if Chordata hadn't politely said it was time for the younger elephants to nap, and told me to come back tomorrow.

I was brought out of my reverie as an elderly woman

standing on the porch of the shanty we were walking by suddenly leaned out and clutched my arm.

"You're not from around here!" she said. *"Who are you? Where do you hail from, boy?"*

When I turned around, Bem and Kulay were running full speed down the alley.

"There was a rumor that an alien person escaped from Ergent Seth's starship," she said. "He sent you, didn't he? Now he's sending spies, is that it?"

"I'm not a spy," I said.

"Like you wouldn't lie to me if you were."

I yanked back my arm, trying to break her steely grip. Suddenly she slapped me across the face.

Which was crazy, because the hand that she wasn't clutching me with never moved from the porch railing.

The old lady had smacked me with her mind, I realized.

"Where do you think you're going?" she demanded.

Her head jerked as I mentally slapped her back. I felt a little bad, but I had to. I needed to get out of there in a hurry.

I was half a dozen steps down the alley where Bem and Kulay had run when I found myself stuck in place.

I couldn't move.

Chapter 73

THE OLD LADY came hobbling quickly down off the porch and caught up with me. I could feel energy crackling off her, holding me still. A terrible light filled her ancient blue eyes.

Great, out of all the beaten-down citizenry, I had to tick off the one that had powers.

"Bem and Kulay—front and center," the old woman called out.

The two kids came out from behind a stack of pipes and approached the woman meekly.

"Yes, Doctor," they said in unison.

"Who is this odd, renegade person?" she said. "Where did you meet him?"

"Deep in the northern tunnel, Doctor," Bem said. "He said his name is Daniel."

I unfroze suddenly as the dreadful light faded from the old woman's eyes.

I did a double take as she burst into the most incredible girlish laughter. It was quite charming, actually, as if she were both eighty-four and fifteen at the same time.

"Bem and Kulay, you may go," the old doctor woman said, suddenly friendly. "My, my, my. Daniel, is it? You're a real curiosity, aren't you? I was beginning to wonder if any more of your type existed in our poor, poor world. A curious young man. Come from afar, by your looks. And the way you speak. I knew a curious boy like you once upon an age. A boy very much like you. His name was . . . Let me try to remember. Oh, yes. Graff."

Graff! I thought. *You have got to be kidding me!* That six degrees of separation thing even worked in space! Graff had been my father's name!

"Graff? You knew a boy called Graff?" I blurted. "That was my father's name, and he was from your world."

Could it be the same person? I thought. *No. No way.* But the old woman seemed to read my mind. Her wrinkled face appeared to instantly lose twenty years, and she broke into the loveliest smile.

"I knew I sensed something curious and good about you, *son of Graff*," she said, putting a warm, soft palm on my forehead. "Thank you. You've helped me remember . . . the way it used to be."

Chapter 74

SO MANY EMOTIONS and questions rose in me at once. Finally I had a real connection to my family.

To who I was.

To what I was put in the universe to do.

And then the most excruciating pain exploded in my stomach! And with it came a fresh flow of blood. I collapsed, bleeding like a stuck pig.

"What happened to you?" she said. "Your stomach? Tell me, before you pass out."

"I was shot," I said between clenched teeth.

"With what? Be precise."

"A 24/24 Opus Magnum."

She pulled up my shirt for a peek. I couldn't stop her if I tried.

"Must have used a delayed frag round," she said, frowning at the blood and my wound. "Tiny charge inside the bullet. Can be activated at a later date. Even by remote control.

"The bad news is that basically you have a bomb inside your stomach. If we don't get it out of you before the charge goes off, it will send shrapnel through all your vital organs, including your heart."

"Beautiful," I groaned. "Okay, you got my attention. What's the good news?"

"It has to heat up first. We have a few minutes. Let's do this."

My eyes bugged as the tiny old woman put her hands under my legs and neck, lifted me up effortlessly, and carried me into her house.

"Let's do *what*?" I asked.

The front room was piled floor to ceiling with beautifully bound books. In the back room, she swept everything off a cluttered work desk, then laid me down flat.

"We need to operate," she said. "Now. Don't give me any lip. I don't want to hear a word."

Operate? Here?! I could see the dust flakes in the air. Not to mention that I was lying in what smelled like spilled coffee, and maybe bacon grease.

"How close is a hospital?" I moaned.

"No time," she said, tapping a finger to her forehead, as if trying to remember something. She turned and took a vial of gross-looking brown liquid from a nearby cabinet. She handed it to me.

"What are you waiting for? Drink it!" she screamed.

Then she smacked it away as I put it to my lips.

"Wait! *Not that!* The light in here is so bad. This one, I think," she said, handing me a new vial. More nasty brown liquid. Maybe motor oil?

"Are you sure?"

"Don't argue! Don't worry, I used to be a surgeon. But I don't remember a darn thing now. Well, maybe you should worry a little." She cackled as she opened a drawer. I saw hits of light—off metal.

As I forced down the foul potion, she placed a worn leather packet onto the desk beside me, then opened it up. "This could work," she muttered. "Worth a chance."

Hey, wait a second! I thought, gaping at the trowel, pruning shears, spading fork, and hand plow that were inside the pack.

"You're going to operate on me . . . with gardening tools?"

"Aren't we picky? Pull up your shirt!" was the last thing I heard before I passed out.

Chapter 75

I WOKE to the gurgle of running water.

The old woman was washing something at a sink in the corner of the room. *Is she doing the dishes?* I thought woozily.

Then I remembered what had happened to me, and wished I hadn't.

I glanced down at my stomach, which was covered with newspaper. Besides the gardening gear on the work-table, I made out a screwdriver and a needle and thread.

A screwdriver? Come on! I thought, quickly looking away, trying to convince myself not to blow chunks.

The tools were all splattered with blood. My blood.

"Well, what do you know?" my elderly home surgeon said. She was wiping her hands on a blood-splattered apron as she came over. "I can't believe it. You're actually alive."

I realized that the room smelled like smoke. The curtains were singed, and there were broken picture frames and chunks taken out of the plaster in one wall.

"What happened?" I said. "The smoke?"

"I managed to get the bullet out of you, but it blew up right when I was trying to toss it out the window. Piece of shrapnel hit my leg. Thank fortune, it was the wooden one. How are you feeling?"

I looked down at the blood-soaked newspapers wrapped around my stomach. Besides the occasional teeth-clenching throb of agony, I actually felt a little better. Clearer in the head somehow. Being alive is fun like that.

"Like a million bucks," I groaned. "Thank you, um . . . I didn't catch your name, Doctor."

"No doctor. Just Blaleen."

"Thank you, eh, Blaleen," I said. "For saving my life. For . . . whatever you did here."

"Ah, don't mention it," she said, glancing at her wrist. "Wait a second. You haven't seen my watch, have you? I was wearing it a . . ."

An expression of horror crossed her face. She turned suddenly and stared at my stomach. "Oh, dear me."

"No," I cried. "Please, no."

She giggled. "Of course not. Just a little surgeon humor."

But enough joking around, Daniel, she said, talking to me mind to mind now. *You need rest. You almost died on the operating table.*

You recognized me before, didn't you? I thought back at her. *What do you know about me?*

I know many things, Blaleen communicated. *I know you were given a human name, because you and your parents were heading to Earth.*

And I know practically nothing, Blaleen. I have so many questions. Who are you? Who are you, really?

A dear friend, she replied, and held a medicine cup to my lips. *Down the hatch now, Daniel.*

I felt extremely tired. I glanced at the broken pictures that had fallen off the wall. My eyelids grew heavier. In one newspaper picture, a smiling young man was holding a trophy. Graff Wins All-City! read the headline.

Graff?! My father? My father as a young man? Why would the old woman have a picture of my—

"You're my grandmother?" I whispered in a voice I reserved for first sightings of the Grand Canyon and such.

"That's right, Daniel, son of Graff," she said, and smiled down on me. "I am your grandmama."

And then I did what I'd been doing far too often lately.

I passed out.

Chapter 76

WHEN I WOKE from my dreams of being chased through Kansas, Oklahoma, and parts of Texas by The Prayer, I almost went into shock for a second time. I'd been moved to an actual bed! With sheets that were—pinch me—clean! That even smelled nice.

I was lying there, soaking up the whole antiseptic, laundry-detergent-commercial vibe, when I sensed there was someone in the room with me.

I slowly leaned over the edge of the bed. And blinked. The cutest little brown-haired girl was sitting on the floor cross-legged. She was staring up at me.

"Hello," I said.

"Ahhhhh!" she squealed. "It speaks!" She jumped up and ran out of the room as if she'd seen a ghost.

I sat up in the bed. I could move, apparently. *Amazing.*

Then I even managed to stand without falling. *I was on a roll.*

I heard some commotion as I stepped out of the room. Voices were coming from downstairs. And—*music?* Very lively and pretty. Like classical mixed up with rock and a little country and a bit of jazz.

I arrived at the top of some stairs and looked down. The lower level of the house, where my surgery had taken place, had been completely transformed. Not only was it cleaned up, but two dozen or so people were sitting, eating, talking, and laughing.

I stared at them, and at a table filled with delicious-smelling food.

Another song started to play. It was like a Mozart melody, only quicker and somehow warmer. Like maybe Bob Dylan had collaborated on it.

When I got to the bottom of the stairs, I saw that my grandmother, Blaleen, was at a kind of piano. Another ancient woman in a wheelchair was playing a small stringed instrument that looked and sounded just like a guqin, a type of ancient Chinese guitar. Seven or eight little kids running around a bunch of chairs scrambled for a seat as the glorious music suddenly stopped.

"Little ones, say hello to your great-cousin Daniel," my grandmother said, standing as she spotted me. "Daniel X, to be precise. He doesn't use a family name because he doesn't have a family. Until *now*, that is."

"There he is!" a pretty young woman cried as she ran up and embraced me. "By the stars, it's true! I'm your cousin Lylah."

For the next several minutes, people crowded around, shaking my hand, patting my back, and pinching my cheeks. Shocked eyes stared into mine and dazed smiles lit up faces. The old woman in the wheelchair rolled up to me. There were tears in her eyes as she pinched my cheek as well.

"It's true," she whispered happily to me. "Ya look just like your mom. Little of your dad. Lovely! Just lovely! You're beautiful, Daniel. Tall, blond. Stunning!"

An amiable-looking, pudgy man was pinching my free cheek. "Daniel, Daniel. Pleasure to meetcha. I'm your uncle Kraffleprog. Your mom's brother," he said, pumping my hand. "I used to change your diaper. *I called you Stinkyboy*."

Kraffleprog? I thought as I shook his hand. Now there's a name you don't hear that much anymore. My parents had taken some serious pity on me in the name department, I realized.

"I can't remember the last time there was a party, can you?" said a bony, tired-looking woman standing beside Uncle Kraffleprog.

"First time in a while we had something to celebrate on this shattered rock," my rotund uncle said, winking and pinching me some more. "Stinkyboy is back."

Chapter 77

"COME, DANIEL. Take the place of honor at our table," my grandmother said. "It's a miracle you lived through my surgery."

The meal, everything, was spectacular, really top of the line. Roast meats, incredibly intense vegetables, a kind of refreshing clear, sweet drink. Alparian apple juice, maybe. I could feel health and heat start to pulse in my veins.

"Grandma," I said, smiling at Blaleen, "your place. It looks . . ."

"Reborn? Yes. Exactly how I feel," she said, squeezing my arm. "Your homecoming defies chance. It has brought back the one thing we thought we would never have again. You know what this is, Daniel? Hope."

Whoa! What was I supposed to say to that?

"Tell me everything," I said, changing the subject. "Who I am. Who the Alien Hunters are. What my parents were doing on Earth. Where—"

"Whoa, whoa! I'll give you the short version, Daniel. Listen now.

"Many hundreds of years ago, our space probes discovered Earth. What amazed us was how similar our planets were, in temperature, atmosphere, bodies of water. It was discovered that the human heart was also similar to that of Alparians; physically, and in other ways as well. It was suggested that our races might have descended from a single ancestor.

"Unfortunately, we soon learned the Outer Ones had already discovered Earth and were working to colonize and take it over. My son, Graff, met and fell in love with your mother, Atrelda, when they were at university. They both had powers, Daniel, telepathy and transforming ability. They could, well, create things at will. It's rare, but it happens here."

"Did you tell him about his rating?" my uncle interrupted.

"You were tested, Daniel. Your powers are double those of your gifted parents *put together*. Graff and Atrelda were sent to Earth to help humans in any way they could. When we learned of their deaths at the hands of The Prayer, we were convinced you had perished as well."

"So tell me—what happened to Alpar Nok? When did Seth destroy it?"

"Not destroyed. Just changed things superficially. But enough of that for now. The past is the past. This is the surprise. This gathering is for happiness and renewal and hope. Everyone, shall we?" my grandmother said. "We have a present for you."

The plates were cleared away and the lights turned low.

"This," said my uncle, "is not to be believed, young Stinkyboy!"

Chapter 78

ALL MY RELATIVES had started to hum. I was about to ask what was up when a flicker of light appeared on the wall.

Then a scene formed.

It was a mom and dad and a little boy in a powder blue rowboat. Hey, wait! That wasn't just any little boy. That was me!

My relatives were projecting some kind of memory home movies on the wall for me! How crazy was that? And how cool.

For the next hour, I rested my chin in my palms and

watched memory after memory in total awe! My mom and dad in what looked like navy officers' uniforms, getting married. Taking me home from the hospital, playing with me in a swimming pool, playing with me at the beach. I smiled as I spotted myself petting Chordata's trunk.

After a while, the scene on the wall changed to me as a small child playing with four friends.

Suddenly it felt like the top of my head blew off! I tapped my grandmother's hand as I realized who this was. *Joe, Willy, Dana, Emma, and me in a sandbox!*

My buds! My dudes! No way! We were good friends even as little kids?

"Wait a second! That's Joe, Willy, Emma, and Dana. My friends," I said excitedly.

"Yes, they were your friends from preschool. My, how you used to get on," my grandmother said. "You formed a friendship bond, called a *drang,* that is rarely seen among our people. Very powerful, Daniel. Very special."

"But where are they now? I have to see them immediately."

She touched my face.

"I'm so sorry," she said. "They were together at the Academy when it was bombed on FirstStrike. Their bodies were never recovered. They're presumed dead, Daniel."

Tears sprang to my eyes as I felt the strength suddenly leave my body. My head hit the tabletop as a bolt of despair shot into my brain stem. It felt like I was being torn in two.

With all the destruction that I had seen, the ruin of an entire world, it wasn't until this moment that I was truly overcome. I hadn't felt such sadness since I was three.

Dana, Joe, Emma, and Willy—my best friends had all been murdered by Ergent Seth and his villains.

I don't know exactly who I was when I finally lifted my head and dried my eyes. Just that I wasn't the same person I had been minutes before.

"Seth," I whispered. "I'm coming for you. I swear I am. I promise you, Dana, Joe, Emma, Willy, my dear dead friends! My *drang*."

Chapter 79

MY HEAD WAS STILL SPINNING when I woke up the morning after the party. Meeting my real family for the first time would have been overwhelming in itself. But at the same time trying to get up to speed on my people *and* the history of my planet and—hello!—my destiny had been like drinking from a fire hose.

I was hoping to catch a few stragglers from the night before. I still had about a thousand questions bouncing around in my skull. But there was no one. In fact even my grandmother seemed to be gone.

I found a handwritten note taped to the inside of the

front door.

Dear Daniel,

You are still recuperating, so I couldn't bear to wake you, but there is grave news! Terrible, woeful news!

The Outer Ones' World Harvesters have reached the outskirts of Undertown, our last sanctuary in the city. A cave-in at one of the lower tunnels has left hundreds of casualties, and I must leave to help. It is utter chaos and desolation for thousands more who have lost their dwelling places. Mothers and children are weeping and bleeding in the streets.

You have come at a miserable, desperate time for our planet. Who knows, maybe this is no accident. The horse-faced beasts are everywhere, so I must go.

I hope to see you again, and if not—

Love, great love, for all of eternity, my brave, handsome Daniel.

Grandma Blaleen

Chapter 80

THE SUN WAS GETTING LOW as I finally made it back out of the confusing maze of tunnels under Alpar Nok's shattered surface. I turned into the nearest abandoned office tower and hit its stairwell at a gallop. Grandma Blaleen was right—the horse-faced beasts were everywhere!

A short time later, I stood on the roof, watching the sun set. The Alparian sun was almost twice as large as Earth's. Or was Alpar Nok just closer to it? Anyway, it had a yellowish-green tinge that turned into a blue and gold as it sank. It was heart-stoppingly beautiful, as I was sure this city had once been. I imagined this same fate for New York and Paris and London back on Earth, and it chilled me to the bone.

Then I stared at Seth's spaceship hovering ominously in the distance. And his sickening machines eating through this planet, like worms through a smashed apple.

I thought about all the dreams and beauty Seth had taken away. And lives—like Joe's, Willy's, Emma's, Dana's. My dear friends murdered long ago at their school, of all places.

How long would it be before this same kind of senseless destruction would be replayed on Earth?

I closed my eyes, concentrated fiercely, and brought my friends back. With my mind, of course.

"Whu-what?" Joe said, coming up beside me. "No! You gotta be messing with my head. I mean, the alien spaceship was a trip, but now we're actually on another *planet*? A wrecked planet, I see, but still. Tell me they have light sabers, Daniel. I want my own light saber!"

"Don't listen to him, Daniel," Willy said, punching Joe in the arm. "He's just taken one small step for idiots, one giant step for idiotkind."

"I know things look bad now, Daniel," Emma said, scanning the jagged horizon. "But this planet has an incredible life force, one that is even greater than Earth's.

I can practically taste it. Given time and isolation, it'll come back."

I felt something hopeful in my chest. I'd almost forgotten how good it felt to be among my friends again. *My murdered friends,* I couldn't help thinking.

I stepped over to where Dana stood, off by herself, looking very sad.

"What is it, Dana? Why won't you talk? Did I do something wrong?"

Her eyes teared. Suddenly she hugged me hard.

"Okay, Daniel, I know what you have to do here. I'm just so afraid, afraid of losing you. And myself. But let's get to work anyway. Let's try to stop Seth if we possibly can."

For the next several hours, we just sat there and thought about how to save our homeland. We turned over the options and possibilities, thousands of them, actually. Unfortunately, they all pretty much stank.

"What do we do now?" Dana finally asked. "We still don't have a plan—and my brain is getting numb."

"Sleep," I said. "Dream about The Prayer, I suppose. But tomorrow we fight to live!"

Chapter 81

THE NEXT MORNING it took us hours of tricky and difficult hiking through the landfill of the destroyed city to get anywhere near Seth's ship.

If the disaster area looked bad from far away, close up it was much worse. There were thousands of horse-heads everywhere I could see.

We staggered around shattered baby cribs, computer screens, old newspapers and books, broken appliances, skeletons, all of it covered thickly with ash and mud.

When we got closer to Seth's gigantic spacecraft, I saw that another landing chute was down.

"I guess he's not afraid of an attack," I said.

"What are we going to do?" Willy said nervously. "I don't like the look in your eyes."

"Get it over with," I said. "Tussle, rumble, duel to the death. Something awful, something final."

I pulled a metal pole out from the rubble. Then I hurled it about the length of three football fields. About four seconds later, the pole clanged against the ship's hull.

"What *are* you doing?!" said Emma as a deafening alarm sounded in the ship.

"Do you see a doorbell anywhere?" I said, and walked forward.

"Knock, knock!" I yelled up at the belly of the ship. "Come out, come out, wherever you are, Seth! It's me. Daniel."

Chapter 82

ABOUT TWENTY SECONDS LATER, there was a metallic groaning sound, and the door opened.

Seth came out in a bathrobe, holding a travel mug of coffee in one hand and a folded-over *Wall Street Journal* in the other. The dozen or so commando soldiers who filed out the doorway behind him swung their 24/24 Opus Magnums in my direction.

"Well, if it isn't Daniel X himself," Seth said with a yawn. "Become tired of living in this dump of a city already, eh? What can I do for you today? Death? Eternal enslavement? What's it going to be?"

"I had something a little more sempiternal and epic in mind," I said as I put my fingers to my mouth and whistled. "You saw *Lord of the Rings I, II,* and *III,* right?"

At first, nothing happened. Then, slowly, there was movement at the rim of the valley wall. Actually, it seemed as if the rim itself was moving, which couldn't be.

Spikes of light glittered off thousands upon thousands of mirrored visors, and titanium battle helmets, and rifle barrels.

Around the edge of the valley walls stood a massive army of futuristic-looking starship troopers. Each soldier was sheathed head to toe in high-tech silver battle armor, and each one aimed a blocky, snub-nosed submachine gun down at Seth and his fellow aliens.

Suddenly their voices roared as one!

I smiled, trying to mask the fact that each and every cyborg space marine had been created by yours truly.

With my mind.

I turned back to Seth as his newspaper fluttered down from his claw. I thought his eyeballs were going to pop out of his butt-ugly face.

"You thought we were all gone, didn't you?" I yelled theatrically. "Thought you had us beaten into submission? Think again. Prepare to feel the terrible wrath of Alpar Nok!"

Dana leaned in from behind me and whispered against my cheek.

"Daniel, will they actually be able to fight?"

"I honestly don't know," I said out the side of my mouth.

"Great," she said. "One more question. Will it hurt when I die?"

Chapter 83

"PREPARE TO FIRE on my order!" Seth screamed to his soldiers. "And summon more backup. I want a full squadron of battle tanks and missile drones! Get me a *million* squadrons!"

"Anybody moves, they're dead. Same goes for you, Seth," I said.

Our eyes locked and held. This was the crucial part of my plan. The next ten seconds or so meant everything, the future of this planet, and probably of Earth. Hey, you can never be too dramatic when you're psyching yourself up before a battle to the death.

"On Earth, this is what they call a Mexican standoff," I said. "You move, you die. I move, I die. So how about instead we actually see who is more powerful: Alien? Or Alien Hunter?"

"What are you saying, Daniel?" Seth said.

"You and I fight man-to-man. Man to *whatever* you are. Winner take all. You win, my warriors disarm and become your slaves. I win, you and your hideous cretins slime back into your flying Dumpster and never come back."

After all my thinking and searching through annals of every strategy and warfare book ever written, I'd actually gotten the ploy from *The Iliad,* by Homer. Achilles gets Hector outside Troy's walled gates to fight him one-on-one while both their armies watch. Check it out in *The Iliad.* Great story!

Seth suddenly laughed at me.

"Sounds exciting, except I really don't care how many of my drones die. How about I just give the fire order and go back and watch the end of *24,* the fifth season, on my DVD?"

"Oh, I get it now," I said, shrugging. "Seth is afraid of a fifteen-year-old. I'm not surprised."

"What did you just say?" Seth said, putting a claw to his ear.

"You heard me. *Gutless. Ugly. Slime-bucket. Horse-headed beast.* How can I put it any clearer? Let's see. You're totally petrified of me? You're quaking in your bedroom slippers? You just soiled your undies with the little hearts on them? Isn't that right, *Dumb-Dumb?*

Seth, already halfway inside the door of the ship's elevator, stopped suddenly. "*Dumb-Dumb,*" he muttered.

"Hold this," he said, handing his coffee, paper, and robe to one of his hench-creeps.

"Bring down the Earth slaves!" Seth roared. "Watching the death of this fledgling *nothing* will be a once-in-a-lifetime learning experience for them."

I resisted the urge to wipe sweat from my forehead, and just about everywhere else on my body.

My plan was working so far, I guessed. I'd used what I'd learned from Seth's dream to manipulate him. In the dream, he was a little mutant horse-head, and all the other horse-heads were chanting "Dumb-Dumb" at him while he was being humiliated by a horse-head teacher.

Being thought dumb was Seth's greatest fear. *Join the crowd.*

And mine? Maybe being torn limb from limb by one of the strongest and most evil creatures in the known or *unknown* universes.

Chapter 84

TEN MINUTES LATER, the sun was blazing directly over our heads, and all the Earth kids were watching with google eyes. The scene reminded me of the Roman Colosseum, or at least the way it looked in *Gladiator*.

Seth's clawed feet made nails-on-a-blackboard scratching sounds as he approached across the courtyard of our makeshift arena.

Me and my big yap, I thought. Defeat Number 6? I doubted I could last thirty seconds with the beast.

That's when Joe started his ridiculous ringside announcement.

"Ladies and gentlemen. And all of Seth's creeps," Joe shouted. "In this corner, wearing Eagle Outfitter jeans and a powder blue Gap T-shirt, weighing in at one hundred and forty pounds—Daniel, the Wailin' Alien."

By this time, along with the Earth kids, what seemed like everyone surviving on Alpar Nok, including my aunts and uncles and my grandmother, had arrived on the scene. They'd held back at first—probably as frightened as I was—but now they were cheering like a home crowd at Dodger Stadium.

"And in the nether corner, standing seven and a half feet tall and weighing in at a whopping six hundred ninety pounds, and maybe more—Ergent 'The Planet Eater' Seth."

I turned and stared at Joe.

"Would you shut up already?" I said. "You're making him angry."

"*Angrier,*" Seth corrected. "Just wait till you see *angriest.*"

"Sorry," Joe said sheepishly. "I always wanted to do that. It was *great!*"

"Fair warning, sir," I babbled as Seth got closer and closer. "Did I tell you? My powers came back. In full. And maybe some extra since I'm now well rested."

Bluish light crackled from my fingertips as I spun to my left. Then an enormous wall of energy flew up, protecting the Earth children from any kind of harm.

Seth threw up one hand—the energy wall I'd created buckled and disintegrated with a loud sucking sound. The Earth kids were left unprotected again.

"You were saying something," Seth said, holding a claw over his mouth as he yawned.

"Oh, I get it," I said. "I'm the one who creates, you're the one who destroys. Interesting concept."

"Isn't it, though?" Seth said as he rushed forward to end my life.

Chapter 85

I LET HIM keep coming until the last possible second, when I dropped low and tumbled directly under his legs. I even managed to hook my right foot around his leg and trip him.

The home and away crowd cheered as he landed hard enough to crack the stone ground.

Okay, I thought. *So far, so alive.*

Seth grunted as he got up and shook his mammoth shoulders. He jogged toward me, then stopped and grinned. He curled his claws, crouching in a kind of kung fu stance.

I put up my fists beside my head and crouched, waiting for the next, furious attack.

But instead of the roundhouse kick I was expecting, a forked bolt of red lightning erupted out of Seth's mouth. It struck me point-blank in the forehead.

Not fair, I thought, as sizzling force and blinding light hit me between the eyes like a burning sledgehammer. *Nobody said anything about lightning.*

I stumbled back, my hair singed, my clothes black and smoking. So much for my *Iliad* strategy, and my being Achilles the Second, and probably my living until tomorrow morning.

"Nice try, Seth," I said, grinning. Which was a pretty gutsy statement considering that I was about to die.

I even managed to stay on my feet. Alien Hunter rule of thumb: *In the event of near electrocution, stay upright.*

And then Seth changed strategies. He ran over me like a runaway freight train.

Maybe might does make right?

Chapter 86

HE ACTUALLY DROVE ME down *into* the stone ground a few inches. Then he wrapped me in his arms and lifted me above his head. Up close, he smelled like death, and yes, unfortunately, I have experience with that particular odor. Far too much for my tender years.

"Oh, Danny," he said in Phoebe Cook's voice as he drew me to him. "I love it when we hug."

Let me walk you through the being-squeezed-to-death-by-an-alien process. First it feels like a dump truck is sitting on your chest. Then it feels like an aircraft carrier landed directly on you. Black stars begin to cloud your vision. I had never seen or even heard of black stars before. Maybe they were the last thing you got to see on your way to the other side.

"*I am more,*" Seth roared through gritted teeth as he continued to crush me into fine particles. "*I am more.*"

I could feel my bones about to pulverize, my eyeballs ready to pop from their sockets.

I held on as long as I could.

Then I forced a final smile.

"I told you I was smarter than you, Dumb-Dumb. Didn't I tell you?"

Seth looked at me curiously, and in the next instant, everything—Seth, the improvised colosseum, the immovable crushing pressure—*all of it was gone.*

I was on a white sheet.

I'm not talking a regular hospital sheet or something, but an incredibly enormous, billowing white sheet, a virtual desert of a white sheet going off and out of sight in every direction.

I was clinging to it desperately. With my arms and legs and teeth.

My eight, long, segmented, covered-in-an-exoskeleton arms and legs, by the way.

I'd turned myself into a tick.

I was now too small for Seth to squeeze to death. Let's face it. I was so small I doubted Seth could even *see* me.

Chapter 87

I STARTED to turbo-climb the cloth cliff of Seth's white shirt. I was actually on his shoulder blade when I turned and saw his enormous eye staring down at me.

Far off, I watched a claw the size of a two-family house rise toward me. Uh-oh.

Then I jumped! The claw actually brushed my back. It came so close, I almost went flying off Seth altogether.

Almost.

I landed on the side of Seth's head, next to his ear.

And then I held my breath . . . and crawled inside.

YUCK!

It was like the most disgusting cave ever discovered. Right in my path was what looked like a tractor trailer's worth of melted Limburger cheese.

My tick torso doubled over and I started to dry heave. I realized I was standing in Seth's earwax.

Finally, though, I rose up tall—and shouted!

"On Terra Firma, they have a product called Q-tips. You should look into it, Seth," I yelled.

"WHO SAID THAT?" he bellowed as I scampered down the curving corridor of his ear canal.

I didn't stop until I came to a bulging red nodule. It was plugging up the tunnel. Now what?

I shut my eyes and pictured the anatomy of the Vermgypian head from the diagram on my laptop. Having a photographic memory comes in really handy sometimes.

I realized I was staring at his tympanic membrane, or eardrum. *Hmmm.* It parted like a curtain as I cut into it with my fang.

Seth howled, so I must have been doing something right.

Next, I wriggled my way into a chamber called the tympanic cavity. Above me was a repulsive bulging, hanging thing that looked like a giant squid. It was Seth's cochlea, the organ that turns sound into brain signals.

There was a little window in it where a funny-looking bone called the stirrup flickered in and out.

I climbed up and crawled over the stirrup and through the window, into Seth's inner ear.

"I'm still here!" I reassured him. "This is still a fight to the death!"

Chapter 88

The inside of Seth's cochlea was even grosser than his earwax situation. It was filled with this fluid that was . . . ugh, I don't even want to get into it.

I swam through the gook until I reached another opening filled with what looked like yellow spaghetti.

Aha! Just what I was looking for, a gaggle of Seth's nerves. Auditory or vestibular, I wasn't sure, and it didn't matter.

I just needed a way to travel so far into his skull that there'd be no chance for him to get me out. I wriggled into a ductlike nerve, headfirst, and continued on my merry way, spelunking through Seth's head.

For some reason, I don't think Seth was having as much fun as I was. Periodically I would hear him moan things like *no* and *please* and my personal favorite, *mommy*.

"I'm right here, honey!" I called back. "But you know what they say about letting an opponent get inside your head?"

After about five minutes of wriggling, I arrived at more yellowish spaghetti, and clumps of unidentifiable organs that looked important, and rather delicate. By my calculations, I was now in Seth's brain stem, halfway between his medulla oblongata and his pons.

This was the Grand Central Station of Seth's brain, the part that controlled his respiration, his blood pressure, his heart rate.

"Are all the brains of your species this small, Chunk Bucket? Or are you like an exception?" I yelled.

"GET OUT OF MY HEAD!" Seth screamed.

His voice was truly thunderous in the chamber of his skull. The voice of an angry god in an evil temple.

"GET OUT OF MY HEAD NOW OR I'LL BOARD MY SHIP AND BLOW THIS PLANET TO DUST!" he screamed.

And that was different from what he had intended to do in what way?

"You want me out of your head?" I said.

"*YES!*"

"You sure?"

"*YES!*"

"Say please."

"*PLEASE!*"

"Okay," I said. "If you insist. But you won't like it. Ready or not, I'm coming out!"

Chapter 89

I LET OUT a thunderous trumpeting roar, and I mean that literally. My tick legs thickened as my body bulged, expanding at an amazing rate.

Seth had begun to shriek for his *mommy* again.

Then my head hit the ceiling of something spongy, and I slid through tissue and membrane with a wet *pop*.

I blinked in the suddenly bright sunlight, raised my glorious trunk to the sky, and trumpeted again.

Yes, trumpeted!

I'd transformed myself into a glorious elephant! One the size of Chordata.

I towered there for a moment, feeling my elephantness, feeling the power and might and wisdom of everything that was hopeful and alive about Alpar Nok.

Seth was lying on the stone beneath me, and well . . . wow. Seth wasn't doing too well. *Euphemism. Look it up.* Where his head used to be was basically a pool of pale-colored slime.

This piece of garbage who had nearly destroyed my planet had had a large head for sure. But even his head couldn't contain a full-grown elephant.

I trumpeted again, and the kids from Earth and Alpar Nok leaped to their feet, cheering.

The remaining alien commandos stood there in shock as I morphed back into myself.

"You there," I said to the largest and nastiest-looking of them all.

"Me?" The creature cringed, fearfully pointing a claw at himself.

"Yes, you," I said. "What's your name?"

"Krothgark."

"Krothgark, I haven't decided if I'm going to let you live or not. Would you like to influence my decision?"

"Yes," Krothgark said. "Very much."

"Then do yourself a big favor and unchain those kids," I said. "And *those* kids. And *those. All* of them."

"You got it, sir. Right away, right away. You heard the

man," Krothgark said, smacking one of the horse-head soldiers next to him. "Unchain the children."

When I looked up I saw that people were streaming toward me. I gave Bem and his sister, Kulay, high fives as my uncle pinched both of my cheeks.

"*Woooh*," I heard Joe yell from somewhere in the happy crush. "Yeah, baby! We're going to Disney World." Leave it to Joe.

"You've saved us," Grandma Blaleen said as she hugged me tightly.

Then Dana had her arm around me too, and nothing had felt so good to me in a long, long time.

"You're . . ." she sobbed. "You're . . ."

"Still alive?" I said. "Of course. How could I let *us* die?"

Just then, a human girl came running up to us. She had flaming red hair, lots of freckles—very pretty. "I was held captive on that terrible spaceship," she said. "Thank you for saving me. I'm Phoebe Cook, the real one."

She had something tucked under her arm. "I found this on the ship. I thought it might be important."

My laptop! I reached for the computer containing The List of all the other alien scum I had to destroy, but before I could say a word to Phoebe, Dana did.

"It's very nice to meet you, Phoebe. I'm glad you're all right. Now you should go back and celebrate with your friends. Daniel is with me. Bye-bye, Phoebe. Scoot along."

Chapter 90

IF I THOUGHT the first feast at my grandma's was something, I hadn't seen anything yet. There were twelve straight days of dancing and music, celebrating, eating, storytelling, you name it. Except that you couldn't possibly imagine a blowout party on Alpar Nok, could you?

For hours and hours, total strangers came up and embraced me. My arms were sore from shaking hands. And my cheeks, from being pinched. I was told that I met every single inhabitant of Alpar Nok. *Twice.*

At one point during the final fireworks show—*really,*

this was the final—I found my grandma and sat her down for a heart-to-heart.

"Let me help you rebuild the city," I said. "Where do we start? When?"

"No," she said, shaking her head. "You've done enough here, Daniel. You have to go back to Earth. Finish the work your parents started. And I'd go *now,* if I were you. Make the Outer Ones take you and the rest of the abducted kids back. Before those blackguards can think about it, and do something deceitful and treacherous."

"But when will I see you again?" I said. "*Will* I see you again?"

"Of course you will, Daniel," she said. "In your dreams, in your mind's eye, and always in your heart."

"One question," I finally said. "Seriously now. Are you a doctor?"

She shrugged. "Gardener," she said.

Epilogue

KISSING THE EARTH WITH MY DRANG AND ALL THAT GOOD STUFF

Chapter 91

THE SUN WAS JUST STARTING to set as we crossed a cornfield near Huxley, Iowa, where I had the Outer Ones drop us off after we'd delivered the last of the abducted Earth children safely home. I was watching the departing spaceship when I almost tripped over a football lying in the grass.

You wouldn't think that a scuffed-up, oblong ball with *nfl* written in jazzy script under its laces could actually fill a person with unbridled joy, but I almost started crying.

Something good had just happened. I was back on

Terra Firma, and I'd missed it like crazy, more than I ever could have imagined.

This is my home, I realized. *I love it here. It's a great, great planet.*

I bent and lifted the football.

"Joe," I said, hefting it. "Go long, my man."

Willy, Dana, Emma, and I cracked up as we watched Joe run. Fewer things in life are funnier than watching Joe-Joe put the pedal to the metal. When he got about eighty yards away, he yelled back.

"I'm open, Daniel! Throw it! Chuck it! Montana to Jerry Rice, Brady to Randy Moss, Brett Favre to anybody!"

"You call that *long?*" I yelled at him.

Joe kept running, and talking. About four minutes later, when he was basically a blip on the horizon, my cell phone rang.

"This long enough for you, wise guy?" Joe said, breathing heavily into the phone.

"That'll do it," I said, and let the football fly. It made a hissing sound through the golden, early evening sky as it spiraled toward Joe and the sun. I was glad there weren't any passing aircraft, because I had to put some arc on that sucker.

Joe was standing about half a mile away. We burst into loud applause as he caught it and then got knocked onto his butt.

"Now that's what I call a catch, Joe," I said as I ran up and saw my bud sitting smack-dab in the middle of a cow pie. Willy was punching his thighs, he was laughing so hard.

"And check it out," I said, pointing toward the field behind Joe. *"We're not the only ones impressed."*

Chapter 92

THERE WERE COWS in the field, a herd of black-and-white Holsteins. Joe's mouth went wide as the moo-cows stood on their hind legs with their hooves at their waists.

With a little help from me, of course. My last trick of this story, I swear.

"Give me a *J!*" I yelled.

"Moooo," the cows bawled, and made a *J* with their front hooves.

"Give me an *O!*"

The hooves made an *O*.

"Moooo!"

"Give me an *E!*"

Thirty Holsteins bent sideways, their front hooves and one rear hoof extended. *Very cool to watch.*

"Mooooo!"

Even Emma, who rarely approved of doing anything with animals except setting them free, looked like she was about to wet her pants with the excitement.

The grand finale of the routine came as they assembled in a four-base cheerleading pyramid. The two Holsteins at the top had extended their hooves skyward.

"What does it spell?" we all yelled out.

"MOOOOO!" the cows bawled as they did these totally impossible cheerleader jumps and basket catches and back handsprings.

My sides were aching from laughing so hard. It was good to be on Terra Firma. And to have my powers again.

"Be afraid, aliens," Dana said, hopping up on my back, pumping her fist at the sky. The sun was dipping over the rise of the country road in front of us. I began to run faster and faster and faster. You wouldn't believe how fast.

"Be very, very afraid!" I screamed to this blurring, wonderful world of ours.

A look ahead to further adventures
(if you want to peek)

One

IT WAS A PRETTY REGULAR early summer night at 72 Little Lane. The crickets and katydids were making that soothing racket they make on warm, still, small-town evenings. The back porch light was on, but otherwise the tidy brown house was happily, sleepily dark.

At least it was until 11:35, when the local news came to an end, and a few TV sets in homes further down the street began to play the opening skit of a popular comedy show. At that point all the insects fell silent, silent as the grave—and not because it was their bedtime or because they'd gone off to watch TV.

They had succumbed to a silent command. It's hard to exactly translate the command—it couldn't be heard by human ears and the language of insects isn't one that easily can be put into words anyhow—but every six-legged creature in the area instantly decided it was a very good time to hide under a rock, wedge into the tree bark, or even dig a little ways down in the dirt . . . and to be very, *very* quiet.

And then, inside the small brown house, it became very, *very* loud. Every speaker—on the computers, on the television sets (the one in the den was a brand new flatscreen with THX surround-sound) on the cell phones, on the iPods, on the radios, on the telephones, even on the "intelligent" microwave—began to blast a dance song from a popular old movie, a dance that was a favorite of a very slimy, very fat, very fishy-smelling, and very *powerful* alien.

Two

THE BOY FUMBLED FOR his clock radio. It was blaring some super-lame old 70s song by one of those awful disco bands his mom sometimes played in the car. His sister must have changed the station as a prank. He'd get her back—later, in the morning—when he'd had some sleep.

He punched the snooze button, but it didn't shut off. He flicked the switch on the side, but it didn't shut off. He picked the clock up off his bedside table and saw that it was just past 11:30 *at night*.

She was going to pay for this. He reached down and pulled the cord out of the socket . . . but it still didn't shut off.

"What the?!" he said, and rubbed his eyes with his free hand. The clock was no longer telling the time; the glowing display now read, "DANCE."

And then a new disco song began and a voice loud and screechy enough to cut through all the noise said: "DO THE DANCE!"

"Now *that's* freaky," said the boy, and he started to get scared. Only he wasn't scared for long because a blue spark leapt out of the alarm clock and up his arm, and suddenly all he cared about was getting downstairs to dance.

He ran out of his room and collided with his father in the hallway. And now his mom and sister were pushing at him from behind and the entire family almost killed themselves tumbling down the stairs to the living room.

It was weird, thought the boy, because he was pretty sure he hated dancing. Just last weekend he'd refused to join his mom and a bunch of girl cousins at a wedding.

But now he couldn't stop himself. He pushed to the center of the living room and somehow he knew exactly what moves to make, and—except for the look of terror in his eyes—he boogied his heart out like a pimply, pajama-wearing John Travolta.

His mom, dad and sister didn't look like they were having too much fun, either.

In fact, the only fun in the house was being had by the

five monsters watching the family from behind the weird, vein- and slime-covered lights, microphones, and multi-lensed video cameras in the adjoining dining room.

They were laughing their heads off—some of them literally rolling on the floor in amusement.

The boy had a vague urge to stop and stare at these uninvited guests, but it was like there was some new part of his brain that wouldn't let him think about them, even though they were right there—*filming his family*.

He didn't even wonder what it meant when one of the monsters, slapping one of its six scaly knees said, "By Antares, they're good. It's just like Saturday Night Fever!"

And then the one in charge—the fat one in the folding canvas chair, cradling the bullhorn in his left tentacle—replied, with a sigh, "Yes, it's almost a shame we have to *terminate* them."

Three

THE FIVE ALIENS SCUTTLED and hovered out of the TV news van and stared in through the big plate-glass windows of the Holliswood Diner.

They were ugly buggers—three were basically overgrown cockroaches with blue, bald, little-old-man heads; one was like a big, white, angora-furred gorilla (except that he had excellent posture, was really sweaty, and had a rather unfortunate big pink hog's nose); and then there was the one in charge—basically a legless, levitating, thousand-pound sumo wrestler with tentacles for arms, no neck, the head of a catfish, and a thick coating of slime.

"Business is about to pick up *a lot*," said the boss alien, observing the young blond waitress reading a Sherman Alexie paperback at the counter. He grabbed the pig-nosed ape's cell phone, held it to the side of his wide, earless head, and watched as the girl reached across the counter to pick up the diner's phone.

A little spark flashed where his tentacle gripped the cell phone and another leapt out of the phone the girl was holding, arcing straight into her ear. She put down the phone and opened the door for them—eyes glassy, face expressionless.

"What did the Zen Buddhist say to the hot dog vendor?" asked Catfish Head as she showed them to their booths, already chuckling to himself at the coming punch line.

"Make me one with everything!" said the waitress, robotically.

The monsters burst into laughter.

"Actually, on second thought, Sweetie," said Catfish Head, "Why don't you go and make us *everything* with everything. Chop-chop!"

"Good one, boss!" said the pig-nosed ape, stealthily snatching his cell phone back from where his employer had rested it on the table. He carefully wiped it down with a napkin before putting it back in his purple belt-clip.

The girl, meantime, had flown into motion as if

somebody had hit the x2 button on her remote control. She prepared and delivered the aliens heaping stacks of eggs, bacon, sausage, Belgian waffles, sundaes, gyros, coffee, bagels, turkey platters, Cokes, muffins, burgers, cheesesteaks, cheesecakes, clam chowder, oatmeal, root-beer floats, gravy fries, banana cream pies, meatloaf slices, onion rings, mashed potatoes, orange sodas, chicken-fried steaks, oyster crackers, saltines, and basically everything the diner had.

"Careful or you'll burn her out, boss," said the pig-nosed ape.

"Plenty more where that came from. What'd our orbital sensors say the count was now at? 6 *billion* of them?"

He laughed a laugh that sounded like somebody blowing bubbles in turkey gravy.

Four

YOU KNOW THE second-coolest of all my super-powers? It's the one that lets me hear *any* song I've *ever* heard as loud as I want, as often as I want, and anytime I want. It's like I have an iPod implanted in my head. Only, of course, the sound quality's better. And it holds more songs. *Way* more songs. Like *terabytes* more. And, of course, it never needs to be docked or recharged.

The song I was playing over and over again right then, as I motorcycled down I-80, was "Don't Fear the Reaper" by Blue Oyster Cult. I know it's ancient and kinda puts the K in Klassic Rock, but it's a good one. And it was going along real well with my thoughts and plans—thoughts and plans wherein I am the Grim Reaper of bad aliens, the Grim Reaper of very, *very* bad aliens.

I leave the good ones alone, of course. There are a few of them around, too, though not so much on Earth. I mean there's me and then there's . . . well, honestly—and not to bum you out—I've only bumped into a couple other good aliens here on your Big Blue Marble.

But what's the coolest of my super powers, you ask? The way I can smell alien sweat from ten miles away even speeding along a highway with my helmet on? The way I've recently learned to make high-performance, hybrid-engine racing cycles that can drive 3,000 miles at 75 miles per hour on a tank of gas? The way I can pop a wheelie on . . . my *front* wheel?

Well, that's almost un-top-able, it's true, but, no, the coolest of my superpowers is the one with which I can cause my best friends—Willy, Joe, Emma and Dana—to show up *out of my imagination*.

Pretty sweet, no? I mean name a movie or comic-book super hero who can do that—create *real people*?

Five

OF COURSE IT TAKES some concentration and I have to be rested and not taking any allergy medicine, but, really, being able to shoot fireballs or out-race locomotives is nothing next to being able to make friends . . . *out of thin air*.

And they're not bottom-of-the-barrel specimens, either. Joe is basically a life-support device for the world's fastest-moving mouth. He's either chewing his way through some mountain of food that looks to weigh half as much as his skinny butt, or he's talking a blue—and totally hilarious—streak. Oh, and he's good with videogames and computers and things like that.

Emma is our moral compass. While the rest of us are

bent on destroying Outlaw Aliens because we just kind of hate them, the part that gets her worked up is that they're on Terra Firma and doing harm not just to people, but to Nature. Mother Earth has no better advocate than her Birkenstock-wearing self.

Emma's older brother is Willy. He's about my age and is the ultimate wing man. He's built like a brick and slightly harder to scare than one, too. When it comes to squaring off with the members of The List, you couldn't ask for a better intergalactic crime-busting partner. Plus, he's more loyal and steadfast than, like, Batman's butler Alfred, Sam in the Lord of the Rings, Wesley in The Princess Bride, and King Arthur's horse combined. And he's kinda mechanically gifted, so when it comes to weapons and engines and stuff like that, he tends to be our go-to guy.

Finally, Dana is, well . . . I'm probably not going to be able to give you a very objective description, even if I am the one who created her. Let's just say she's got straight platinum blonde hair, is about my age, and somehow manages to be both the most attractive and the most grounded person I've ever encountered.

And I haven't exactly been operating out of a Montana shack all these years.

Oh—and this goes for all four of them—they happen to be *outstanding* at don't-try-this-at-home motorcycle stunts. Like leaning into each other in pairs so they make temporary "cars," with four wheels between them. Or chasing up after an eighteen-wheeler and veering over suddenly, leaning the bikes almost over on their sides and zipping *under* the trailer—behind wheels seven, eight, nine and ten and in front of wheels eleven through eighteen—and coming out safely on the other side.

We did a bit of that and some other stuff you'd normally only see in high-budget movies before finally pulling up to a small-town diner where I was about to face off with the most powerful alien I'd ever engaged in mortal combat. In fact, though I couldn't yet see him, I could smell his fishy disgustingness all over the parking lot—like somebody had left a herring-salad sandwich in a hot car. . . *for a week.*

"Sorry about this," I said to my friends.

"Sorry for what?" asked Joe.

"This is between me . . . and #5." I said.

"You're such a boy," said Dana, hand on her hip, a look of concerned disapproval on her face. "Are you sure you're ready to go that high up the List? No offense, Daniel, but you got pretty lucky with #6"

"Always with the pep-talks, Dana. Thanks a lot."

Then I clapped my hands and she and the rest of them flickered out of existence. (I actually don't need to clap, but it looks cool.) And then I cleared my head for battle.

Six

HIS STENCH WAS bad outside but it was nothing compared to how it was inside the diner. This guy made low tide smell like Obsession for Men. And he wasn't even *in* there any longer.

I must have missed him by just a matter of minutes—the gobs of slime in the booth where he'd been sitting hadn't even skinned over—but he and his henchbeasts had gotten while the getting was still good.

With these higher-up-the-List baddies, I was discovering an unfortunate trend in which they often seemed to know I was coming. I guess I should take it as flattery that they didn't want to run into me, but it was more than a little frustrating to keep bringing my A-game, and then find nobody to play it with.

Anyhow, I knew I'd have to pick up their trail as soon as I could but, for the time being, the important thing was to give some attention to the waitress they'd left behind.

The poor girl was collapsed like a rag doll on the floor next to the counter. Something about her face reminded me of a burnt-out light bulb, or a kid's toy you'd tried to run on a car battery rather than AAAs.

The name stitched on the pocket of her calico uniform was Judy Blue Eyes and, indeed, her eyes were blue—the kind of blue a guy could look into and see the promise of the whole world. A human guy, I mean.

"Hey, Judy, you okay?"

"Nnnn," she said, consciousness slowly percolating back.

I helped her into a booth and gave her a glass of water.

"Wh-wh'appen?" she slurred.

"Umm. I think some bad characters came in and had a food-fight," I said, only it was worse than that. It looked like there'd been some sort of no-holds-barred riot. Smashed china plates, syrup and salt all over the walls, coffee and soda dripping from the tabletops, puddles of alien slime and pierced, empty jelly packets on the seats, ketchup and mayo on the jukeboxes, Promise spread splatted on the ceiling . . .

"Oh gosh," she said, struggling to sit up and take it all in, "I'm *so-o* fired."

"Nah," I said. "I can give you a hand." And then, like somebody had pressed the x8 button on *my* remote, I zipped around with a broom, a mop, a couple bottles of Windex, a dozen dish rags, a quart of old-fashioned elbow grease, and had the place spic-n-span in no time, literally.

"Man, I'm really out of it," said Judy as I returned to her now gleaming booth. "I mean, did you just clean all that up in, like, ten seconds?"

Boy was she cute. I was trying to think of something clever to say back but I was having this weird—though not totally unpleasant—tightness in my chest and all I could manage was this really lame giggle.

Must be an alien thing.

About the Authors

JAMES PATTERSON is one of the best-known and biggest selling writers of all time. He is the author of some of the most popular series of the past decade: the Women's Murder Club, the Alex Cross novels and Maximum Ride, and he has written many other number one bestsellers including romance novels and stand alone thrillers. He has won an Edgar award, the mystery world's highest honour. He lives in Florida with his wife and son.

MICHAEL LEDWIDGE is a novelist who has coauthored two number one bestsellers with James Patterson. He lives in New York City.

James Patterson has taken a few minutes away from his writing to tell us some more about *The Dangerous Days of Daniel X*.

Can you tell us a little about *The Dangerous Days of Daniel X*?

Daniel X, I love as a series. It starts out in a little farmhouse and this kid is like three years old and he's playing with a tic, a little bug, on the floor. You know there is something weird about this kid because he knows the entire biological make-up of this creature. Then you hear this explosion in the house and you know something bad is going to happen. This seven-foot tall, very scary alien walks down the stairs. But this three-year-old kid has powers and he turns himself into the tic and escapes in the hair of the alien. And that's just in the first pages of the prologue.

The amazing thing about Daniel is that he has what I think is the super power of all super powers: he can create. In the first chapter, he is fifteen, he has grown up, he has inherited the job from his father to hunt aliens – you may not know this, but there have been aliens on the earth for millions of years. He has just hunted down an alien in the city and he hears noise outside and it is truant officers: people who come after kids who don't go to school and the neighbours have been complaining because he's out to all hours of the night and stuff. So he opens the doors to the truant officers and what happens then is every kid's dream: he brings in his parents and says 'Well talk to them, I'm not a truant,' and his parents talk to these truant officers in a very irreverent way to the point where they just leave the room, leave the house and then Daniel disappears his parents: he created his parents just to deal with these truant officers. The book is full of these very imaginative uses that he makes of the powers that he has, especially this ability to create.

Where did the idea for *Daniel X* come from?
Oh man, where did the idea for Daniel X come from? I've had the idea for a long, long time but I just didn't quite know what the story was going to be. This notion of a kid or a person who can create is just so irresistible to me. It's just the ultimate story device; it's just so cool for storytelling that somebody can create like this. It's also about creativity, how do you solve problems? Usually you solve them with creativity so that's really what underlies *Daniel X*.

Tell us more about the *Daniel X* series
The first full book is obviously published and what we are going to do next is a graphic novel of the second book and that has been illustrated by a fella in Sweden who's

wonderful. It looks great; it's one of the best looking graphic novels I have ever seen. So the second story will be done in that form and then the third will be done in traditional book form again. The third one actually takes place in England, in London.

How do you write the books?
I tend to start with the idea and then I research it so for *Daniel X* I had to meet a lot of aliens and interview them and talk about what they are capable of doing. For *Maximum Ride* I actually had to fly.

Who is the ideal audience for your books?
Anybody who's old enough to read a novel, but not so old they can't see any longer... or have fooled themselves into thinking they don't like page-turning thrillers.

How did you come to start writing books for young adults?
I guess I started writing books like this because I've never grown up; I don't want to grow up. When I write a story, I pretend there is somebody sitting across from me and I tell them a story and I don't want them to get up until I am finished. My theory about getting people to read is that the best way to do that is to give them books that they just can't put down. The pages turn themselves

Where do you write the books?

I have an office in my house and it's actually quite nice because it has a view of the Hudson River so it's very beautiful and peaceful. Somebody said you are lucky if you find something you like to do as an adult and then it is a miracle if somebody will pay you to do it and that is what I have, I love what I do, I love telling stories. I look forward to getting up every morning to work, to tell stories.

How do you write?

Unfortunately I am a dinosaur; I write with a pencil, I do not use a computer. I write, I erase, I write some more. It's kind of silly but it has worked for me and you know that old saying, 'if it isn't broken, don't fix it.'

Who is the first person to read the books?

My son, Jack, is nine. He is a good reader and has read all the *Maximum Ride* books and he likes them very much (or I won't feed him!) and he loves *Daniel X*. Usually he'll say 'It's pretty good dad,' but he really loves *Daniel X*, he gave it an A+.

Don't forget to check out www.daniel-x.co.uk and www.jamespatterson.co.uk for all the latest news.

Read on for a thrilling extract of
James Patterson's

The Final Warning

CATCHING BIRD FREAKS: HAZARDOUS DUTY AT BEST

1

Windsor State Forest, Massachusetts

Ssssss.

The soldiers' armor made an odd hissing noise. But besides the slight sound of metal plates sliding smoothly, flawlessly over one another, the troop was unnaturally quiet as it moved through the woods, getting closer to the prey.

The faintest of beeps caused the team leader to glance down at his wrist screen. Large red letters scrolled across it: ATTACK IN 12 SECONDS . . . 11 . . . 10 . . .

The team leader tapped a button, and the screen's image changed: a tall, thin girl with dirt smears on her face and a tangle of brown hair, glaring out at him. TARGET 1 was superimposed on her face.

. . . 9 . . . 8 . . .

His wrist screen beeped again, and the image changed to that of a dark-haired, dark-eyed, scowling boy. TARGET 2.

And so on, the image changing every half second, ending finally with a portrait of a small, scruffy black dog looking at the camera in surprise.

The team leader didn't understand why Target 7 was an animal. He didn't need to understand. All he needed to know was that these targets were slated for capture.

. . . 3 . . . 2 . . . 1 . . .

The leader emitted a whistle pitched so high that only his team members could hear it. He motioned toward the small run-down cabin they had surrounded in the woods.

Synchronized perfectly, as only machines can be, the eight team members shouldered eight portable rocket launchers and aimed them straight at the cabin. With a *whoosh,* eight large nets made of woven Kevlar strands shot out from the cannons and unfolded with geometric precision in midair, encasing the cabin almost entirely.

The team leader smiled in triumph.

2

"THE PREY HAVE BEEN CAPTURED, SIR," the team leader said in a monotone. Pride was not tolerated in this organization.

"Why do you say that?" the Uber-Director asked in a silky tone.

"The cabin has been secured."

"No. Not quite," said the Uber-Director, who was little more than a human head attached by means of an artificial spinal column to a series of Plexiglas boxes. The bioengine that controlled the airflow over his vocal cords allowed him to sigh, and he did. "The chimney. The skylight."

The team leader frowned. "The chimney would be impossible to climb," he said, accessing his internal encyclopedia. Photographs of the prey scrolled quickly across the team leader's screen. Suddenly an important detail caught his attention, and he froze.

In the corner of one of the photographs, a large feathered wing was visible. The team leader tracked it, zooming in on just that section of the image. The wing appeared to be attached to the prey.

The prey could fly.

He had left routes of escape open.

He had failed!

The Uber-Director closed his eyes, sending a thought signal to the nanoprocessors implanted in his brain. He opened his eyes in time to see the team leader and his troop vaporize with a crackling, sparking fizzle. All that was left of them was a nose-wrinkling odor of charred flesh and machine oil.

Part One

ANOTHER PART OF THE BIG PICTURE

3

A DIFFERENT FOREST. Not telling you where.

Okay, it doesn't take a genius to figure out that funerals suck. Even if you didn't know the person, it's still totally sad. When you did know the person, well, let's just say it's much worse than broken ribs. And when you just found out that the person was your biological half brother, right before he died, it adds a whole new level of pain.

Ari. My half brother. We shared the same "father," Jeb Batchelder, and you can believe those quotes around "father."

I'd first known Ari as a cute little kid who used to follow me around the School, the horrible prison–science facility where I grew up. Then we'd escaped from the School, with Jeb's help, and to tell you the truth, I hadn't given Ari another thought.

Then he'd turned up Eraserfied, a grotesque half human, half wolf, his seven-year-old emotions all askew inside his chemically enhanced, genetically modified brain. He'd been turned into a monster, and they'd sent him after us, with various unpredictable, gruesome results.

Then there had been that fight in the subway tunnels beneath Manhattan. I'd whacked Ari's head a certain way, his neck had cracked against the platform's edge . . . and suddenly he'd been dead. For a while, anyway.

Back when I thought I had killed him, all sorts of sticky emotions gummed up my brain. Guilt, shock, regret . . . but also relief. When he was alive, he kept trying to kill us—the flock, I mean. Me and my merry band of mutant bird kids. So if he was dead, that was one less enemy gunning for my family.

All the same, I felt horrible that I had killed someone, even by accident. I'm just tenderhearted that way, I guess. It's hard enough being a homeless fourteen-year-old with, yeah, *wings*, without having a bunch of damp emotions floating all over the place.

Now Ari was dead for real. I hadn't killed him this time, though.

"I need a tissue." Total, our dog, sniffled, nuzzling around my ankles like I had one in my sneakers.

Speaking of damp emotions.

Nudge pressed closer to me and took my hand. Her other hand was over her mouth. Her big brown eyes were full of tears.

None of us are big criers, not even six-year-old Angel, or the Gasman, who's still only eight. Nudge is eleven, and Iggy, Fang, and I are fourteen. *Technically,* we're all still children.

But it takes a lot, and I mean a whole lot, to make any of us cry. We've had bones broken without crying about it. Today, though, it was like another flood was coming, and Noah was building an ark. My throat hurt so much from holding back tears that it felt as though I'd swallowed a fist of clay.

Angel stepped forward and gently tossed a handful of dirt onto the plain wooden box at the bottom of the big hole. A hole it had taken all of us three hours to dig.

"Bye, Ari," she said. "I didn't know you for very long, and I didn't like you for a lot of it. But I liked you at the end. You helped us. You saved us. I'll miss you. And I didn't mind your fangs or anything." Her little voice choked, and she turned to bury her face against my chest.

I stroked her hair and swallowed hard.

The Gasman was next. He too sprinkled dirt on the coffin. "I'm sorry about what they did to you," he said quietly. His spiky blond hair caught a shaft of sunlight and seemed to light up this little glen. "It wasn't your fault."

I snuck a quick glance over at Jeb. His jaw was clenched, his eyes full of pain. His only son lay in a box in the ground. He had helped put him there.

Bravely, Nudge stepped closer to the grave and tossed some dirt onto it. She tried to speak but started crying. I drew her to me and held her close.

I looked at Iggy. As if sensing it, he raised his hand and dropped it. "I don't have anything to say." His voice was gruff.

Next it was Fang's turn, but he waved me to go. Total had collapsed in sobs on my shoes, so I gently disengaged him and stepped over to the grave. I had two hothouse lilies, and I let them float onto the coffin of my half brother.

As the flock leader, I was supposed to come up with a speech. There was no way to sum up what I was feeling. I had killed Ari once, then watched him die again as he saved my life. I'd known him when he was a cute little kid, and I'd known him as a hulking Eraser. I had fought him almost to death, and I had ended up choosing him over the best friend I'd ever had. I'd hated everything about him, then found out we shared half of our human DNA.

I had no words for this, and I'm a word *queen*. I've talked my way out of more tight spots than a leopard has, but this? A funeral for a sad, doomed seven-year-old? I had nothing.

Fang came up behind me and touched my back. I looked at him, at his dark eyes that gave away nothing. He nodded and sort of patted my hair, then moved forward and dropped some dirt onto the coffin.

"Well, Ari, I'm sorry that it's ended like this," he said so quietly I could hardly hear him, even with my raptor super—hearing. "You were a decent little kid, and then you were a total nightmare. I didn't trust you—until the very end. I didn't know you much, didn't care to." Fang stopped and brushed some overlong hair out of his eyes. "Right now, that feels like the biggest tragedy of all."

Okay, that so did me in. Mr. Rock being all emotional? Expressing feelings? Tears spilled down my cheeks, and I covered my mouth with my hand, trying not to make a sound. Nudge put her arm around me, feeling my shoulders shaking, and Angel held me tight. Then everyone was holding me, total flock hug, and I put my head on Fang's shoulder and cried.

Daniel X: Alien Hunter
A Graphic Novel

by James Patterson

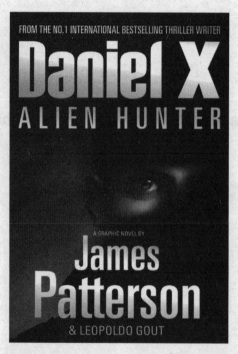

The story of Daniel X, the alien hunter, is brought to life in this brilliantly illustrated, fast-paced graphic novel.

INTRODUCING JAMES PATTERSON'S FAMILY OF PAGETURNERS

'Anybody who's old enough to read a novel, but not so old they can't see any longer can read my books. The best way to get people to read is to give them books that they just can't put down. The pages almost turn themselves.' *James Patterson*

The Final Warning
A Maximum Ride Novel

The Dangerous Days of Daniel X

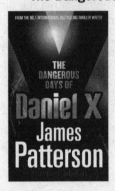

For more information on James Patterson's Family of Pageturners go to:

www.**jamespatterson**.com.au

www.**danielx**.com.au

The Dangerous Days of Daniel X

Daniel X works alone. Having watched from the shadows as the brutal murder of his own parents unfolded before him, he has been forced to make his own way in a dark and unforgiving world with a heavy task handed to him.

Daniel's father was an alien hunter, working his way through a fearsome 'wanted' list of aliens intent on seeking control and wreaking devastation. But as he planned his next target, his own time was running out. Following his parents' sudden deaths, Daniel faced an uncertain future: he knew little about his family nor where he came from but a few things were clear, he had inherited the list from his father and a unique ability to create anything that he needs including some very devoted friends to help him along the way.

His life has become dedicated to the mission. Every day has been transformed into a terrifying hunt, watching each step he takes for danger awaits around every corner and lurks within the shadows. His ultimate aim is to exact revenge against number one on his list: his parents' murderer. But first he must target the others: each more sinister and gruesome than the last.

www.danielx.com.au

The Final Warning

Max, Fang, Iggy, Gasman, Nudge and Angel are six extraordinary avian hybrids. The result of a cruel Biotech experiment which manipulated their DNA and turned them into recombinant life forms with wings. This flock has endured a turbulent upbringing and they have been continually faced with evil. Evading capture on a daily basis, they have endured torture and been pushed to the very brink of sanity.

Hunted all their lives, they've had to fight life-threatening and belief-defying battles pitting their strength against the fearsome force of their shadowy enemies. But as their predators evolved, their unique ability to fly is no longer enough to save them. With their genes mutating to astonishing affect, the flock establishes a new set of skills to unleash as they strive for survival. But just as they struggle to get to grips with these physical changes, emotionally they face new challenges too: life on the fringe of society can be a lonely existence.

Driven to the wastelands of Antartica, each day brings a new threat for the flock. Danger is never far away and while fighting to save their own skin, they have a new mission to undertake – one with devastating global consequences . . .

www.jamespatterson.com.au